Gabe Maxfield never wanted to be a of the sort. The closest he wanted to come was writing briefs and doing research for a big-shot law firm. Nice and safe, and without all the stress. No unanswered questions, just well-defined legal precedents.

When he moves to Hawaii in the wake of a disastrous breakup and betrayal by an ex, a murder investigation is the last thing he expects to get wrapped up in, but he can't help himself when a dead body, a hunky cop, and his best friend get involved.

So much for sipping Mai Tais on the beach and admiring the well-tanned bodies around him.

MAI TAIS AND

MURDER

Gabe Maxfield Mysteries, Book 1

J.C. Long

Published by
NineStar Press
PO Box 91792
Albuquerque, New Mexico, 87199
www.ninestarpress.com

Warning: This book contains sexually explicit content which is only suitable for mature readers, and mentions of violence.

Print ISBN # 978-1-947139-20-6
Cover by Natasha Snow
Edited by Sam Lamb

This book is for Hiro.
You make all the adventures worth it.

Prologue

I NEVER WANTED to be a detective, or a policeman, or anything of the sort. The closest I wanted to come to the law was writing legal briefs and doing research for a big-shot law firm. Nice and safe and without all the stress. No unanswered questions, just well-defined legal precedents. Most of the paralegals I worked with had goals, ambition. Not me; that's the sort of thing that gets a man in trouble.

They said they wanted to be a lawyer—the paralegal thing was experience while they worked on the bar exam. I said *why*? Why would anyone want to put themselves through the hassle of a test that is designed to make you break down in tears? I was safe, never noticed, never standing out, and thus never getting involved in anything big. Boy, was that about to change.

When I moved to Hawaii, a murder investigation was the last thing I expected to get wrapped up in, but you know what they say about the best-laid plans, right? I couldn't help myself when a dead body, a hunky cop, and my best friend got involved.

So much for sipping mai tais on the beach while I admired the well-tanned bodies around me.

Chapter One

THE SOUND OF banging drew me from the nap I'd fallen into on the uncomfortable, lumpy couch I'd inherited in my new condo. I looked around, confused until I realized someone was knocking at my front door rather impatiently.

I hurried across the room, threw open the door, and was greeted with the sight of a burly Islander pulling a dolly loaded up with boxes. The movers were there, finally. I glanced at the watch I wore on my wrist. It was nearly noon, so only, oh, two hours late.

"Aloha, we're with the movers," the man said unnecessarily.

"I thought you were going to be here by ten," I said, stepping out of the door and allowing the man to wheel the dolly inside.

"Yo, you got choke boxes, braddah." It sounded like it was meant to be an explanation, but if it was, I didn't understand it. I'd been in Hawaii for two weeks, and I had not come close to catching on to the local pidgin. I understood what was being said around me about seventy percent of the time, and then suddenly I had no idea. Perhaps he saw the confusion on my face, because he added, not unkindly, "You got a lot of boxes."

I nodded my understanding, deciding not to press the issue of the lateness; I'd learned in my brief time living on the island of Oahu that things in Hawaii ran differently, as if time followed different rules there. Things that would be done at a quick pace back in Seattle just happened slower here—the whole aloha, relaxed island attitude to blame, I supposed. It definitely wasn't a bad thing—in fact, I found the lifestyle here to be worlds better than what I experienced on the mainland. It was just an adjustment. Grace assured me I'd get there eventually, and I was mildly successful already, becoming way more relaxed than I had been in Seattle, but when it came to things like this, I couldn't help but get a little irate.

Didn't people in Hawaii want their packages on time, too? At least pizza delivery still ran on time.

I stood back and allowed the man and his companion to wheel in more boxes. They were about halfway through unloading when the second man stopped and pulled the door down on the back of the truck, leaving the rest of my boxes inside.

"Hey, what are you doing? Those are my boxes!"

"Nevah mine, braddah. Try wait, yeah? We come back bumbye. We gone go grind." The bigger guy came out of the condo behind me, patting my shoulder with a beefy hand.

I ran a hand through my hair. "I'm sorry, I don't quite understand..."

"He said they'll come back in a bit. They're going to get lunch."

I looked over and saw a tall, dark-skinned Islander, bulging muscles all but ripping out of the tight maroon V-neck T-shirt he was wearing. He was about an inch over six feet, with dazzling white teeth and short-cut, dark hair. His eyes were a surprisingly light shade of hazel that contrasted his skin.

"Oh, uh, yeah, okay. Thanks." God, I sounded like a stammering idiot.

If the hunk of an Islander noticed, he didn't say anything. "You've been here a few weeks, right? Why are you just getting boxes? Not that I'm stalking you or anything," he added quickly, eyes widening a bit as he probably processed what he said. Saying you weren't stalking someone made it sound like you were stalking someone. I hadn't taken it that way, but when I thought about it, I could see how it could sound stalker-like. "I live in the condo next to yours." He pointed over my shoulder at the door to his place.

I had my suspicions that he was blushing, but with his face as tan as it was, it was hard to tell. It did look like the skin on the exposed, smooth expanse of his chest and neck had reddened a bit, but was likely just wishful thinking.

That's when I realized I was staring at his chest. Goddamn it, here I was, a twenty-nine-year-old man acting like a fifteen-year-old. "I'm Gabe Maxfield." I introduced myself to establish that I was not, in fact a bumbling idiot. "Nice to meet you."

The guy took my hand and shook it firmly. His touch was surprisingly soft despite the few calluses I could feel, and a warmth spread through me that had nothing to do with the blazing sun. "I'm Maka Kekoa. *Hau'oli kēia hui 'ana o kāua.* That's nice to meet you in *Ōlelo Hawai'i,* the Hawaiian language."

I tried to repeat it, and he smiled at the way I stumbled over the words. "To answer your question," I said quickly, trying to move past the embarrassment of butchering the language, "I wasn't in a rush to get everything since this place came mostly furnished. I shipped them from Seattle at the cheapest—and slowest—rate."

"Oh, you need these guys back here at a certain time?" he asked, gesturing toward the movers, who still hadn't driven off, much to my surprise. They were standing close together, watching our interaction with quite a bit of interest.

"I'm supposed to meet a friend today at three, so they need to be here and finished before then."

Maka nodded and walked to the passenger door of the truck, rapping on it with his knuckles. The door opened and some words were exchanged that I didn't hear—not that I was paying attention. My eyes were too busy traveling over the nice muscles of Maka's arms and the very pleasing shape of his ass.

This was, I realized, the first inkling of physical attraction toward another man I'd felt since things had gone so bad with Trevor two months before. Since then I'd been living in a bit of a fog on many levels, including my libido. I just didn't feel the drive—I couldn't even remember the last time I'd jacked off. Seeing Maka seemed to have poked the bear, so to speak, and I felt myself begin to harden.

I was surprised when the two movers hopped out of their truck, rolled up the back door, and once again started moving boxes. One of them shot a glare at Maka as he went by and muttered something under his breath, but Maka didn't seem to notice.

"How did you do that?" I demanded when he rejoined me.

Maka shrugged, once again flashing those pearly whites. "I have a way with people."

"Clearly. I need to get you to teach me."

"Maybe that can be arranged sometime." Was he flirting with me? Or had I been out of commission so long that I was misreading a simple conversational reply? Why was interacting with a man so complicated? My mind had to go running off in three directions at once, and I didn't even know if this guy played for my team, so to speak. "It was nice to meet you, Gabe. I've got to get going. Tell Pako and his boy that if they have any trouble with anything, they should give me a call, okay?"

"Will do," I said with an awkward chuckle. "Nice to meet you, Maka."

"Aloha."

"Aloha." I waved at him as he left. He'd rounded the corner into a second section of the parking lot when I heard sniggering behind me.

I turned to find the big guy who'd come to my door first—the one Maka called Pako, I think—standing on the porch leaning on the box-loaded dolly, watching me. "What's so funny, exactly?"

"That moke, you gotta be careful," he said, as if that cleared anything up. "He dangerous, you feel? Braddah stay with mad temper."

I looked back in the direction Maka had gone in. "Huh? That guy?"

My ignorance earned me a dismissive gesture. "Mento mahalini be comin' here not understandin' nothin'," he muttered under his breath to his companion who was closing the back of the now empty moving truck.

"Yo, braddah, get the kala," his friend said, nudging him. I wondered what kala meant, but all became clear when he turned around and held out his hand in a universal request for money.

I sighed, dug out my wallet, and shoved a ten into the guy's hand before making my way back inside, not waiting to see if they were going to leave or not. I felt a wave of despair wash over me as I took in the mess that now filled the main room of my small condo. There were nearly twenty boxes—the remnants of my life in Seattle. Seeing them all there made my condo feel claustrophobic. It was like a tower of cardboard shadowing the small couch and cheap off-brand television the place had come with.

The boxes were roughly the same color as the hardwood floors, and they obscured the eggshell-colored walls of the tiny square of the living room. Behind one stack, I could barely see the half bar wall that divided the main room from the kitchen with its slightly different shade of white walls, blue tile floors, and black appliances. It would take me forever to unpack them. At least it would give me something to do during the nights when the doubts and regrets came. I'd taken to fighting them off by watching *Hawaii Five-o* reruns on television, and that could only work for so long, despite how beautiful Daniel Dae Kim was.

I sat down on the lumpy couch and grabbed the box nearest to me, ripping the tape clear and opening it to see what was inside. I closed it right back up, cringing against an emotional jolt. Of course the first box I grabbed would contain the few mementos of my relationship with Trevor. I liked collecting shot glasses, so any time either of us traveled we would get one to add to the collection. Considering Trevor left me with very little, I thought I could at least take the shot glasses.

Looking now at the closed box, I could see that maybe that had been a mistake.

I set the box aside and targeted safer boxes. I'd written "clothes" on all of the boxes that had clothing inside, so I dragged them each—all six of them—into the bedroom and unpacked them. The amount of sweat coating me when I finished surprised me; it was mid-October, after all. However, in Hawaii, it was damn near eighty degrees, and I didn't have my air conditioner on—who needs an air conditioner in October? The windows were thrown open to tempt in the nice Hawaiian breeze, though, and if it weren't for the manual labor of moving the heavy boxes, I would have been fine.

I didn't stop unpacking the boxes and filling up my small closet until my cell phone rang. I dug around on my bed to find it, following the sound. Where was the damn thing? It was an iPhone 6S, and how I could lose something so big when I hadn't left a three-foot radius all afternoon was beyond me.

It went to voicemail before I finally found it inside one of the boxes. How the hell did it get in there?

The missed call was from my best friend, Grace Park—the reason I'd upped my sticks to Hawaii in the first place. In the aftermath of everything that went down with Trevor, Grace was the one who convinced me a change of scenery was in order. I didn't actually require much convincing, though—Seattle had become like a prison for me, sapped of the joy and beauty and warm feelings I once felt toward it—so I couldn't give her all the credit.

I dialed her back, knowing I was going to catch hell for missing the call.

"Hey, Grace, I'm sorry. I was unpacking boxes and couldn't—"

"Sorry for what?" Grace asked over the phone. I knew it was a bait question, as one of her favorite things to do was goad people into admitting fault without her ever having to engage them in an argument. I'd told her on more than one occasion that she should really consider becoming a lawyer; she'd be good at it.

"Nothing," I said quickly. I wasn't going to play her game. "What did you need? Am I late for lunch?"

"No, no. I might be a little late, though." From the sound of it, she was talking to me from her car; I could hear the road and the occasional roar of engines zooming past her. "I got caught up in a photo job."

I snickered. "Hiding in the bushes taking pictures of dirty old men cheating on their wives?"

"No, I was taking pictures of a client's neighbors allowing their dogs to use the client's yard as a toilet without cleaning it up. You'd be surprised how many times it's happened, and by how many different neighbors. Apparently the client isn't well-liked in this neighborhood."

I did not get the appeal of Grace's job. "Sounds...glamorous."

"Glamorous or not, the lady actually paid my steep fee for me to do it. I made three hundred dollars taking pictures of dogs for two hours. I'd say that's a win in anyone's book." I said nothing, because I had to concede her point. "You go to the restaurant, and I'll meet you there as soon as I'm done with my meeting, okay?"

"Sounds fine, I'll—" I stopped talking, though, because she was no longer on the other end of the line. Grace had a really annoying habit of not saying goodbye when she ended a phone conversation, and quite often hung up while the other person was still talking. It was one simple word that took less than a second to say, so she wasn't saving any time. What was so hard about saying "goodbye"?

I considered spending a bit more time unpacking but found the idea to be distasteful, so instead I jumped in the shower to get ready to meet Grace. I hadn't really been out of the house since moving there, except a few times to go grocery shopping or pick up essentials. I hadn't been feeling up to it. Grace, though, had had enough of my moping around and took it upon herself to get me reintegrated with the real world, insisting I meet her for lunch at this place she knew. After browbeating me into accepting, she told me to meet her at the restaurant she took me to on the day I got there for a quick lunch before we hit the rental shop. It wasn't far from my place, so I agreed—reluctantly.

She was right, I knew, which only irritated me. It was about time I got back out into the world. I couldn't live the rest of my life locked away in my condo. Besides, even though it had only been two weeks, I was burning through the money in the trust fund my grandfather left me much faster than I wanted to. It was time for me to return to civilization, get a job, and move on with my life after the disaster that was Trevor. Maybe even find a new man.

The face of my neighbor, Maka Kekoa, flashed through my mind, unbidden, and I turned the shower knob to cold to fight the sudden physical reaction my body had. It was unusual for me to lose so much control of my body; typically, I could will away erections with very little effort. This one, though, even with the needling spray of cold water, persisted.

I needed to leave pretty soon to get to lunch on time, but I didn't want to go to a meeting with Grace while sporting an erection. I turned the shower back to warm and lathered myself up with soap—first concentrating on cleaning and then on making myself feel good.

The intensity of the sensation of my soap-slicked hand on my cock was overwhelming; it had been so long since I'd even touched myself that I could feel the end already approaching. I didn't mind, though. I wasn't looking to draw it out or enjoy it, just get it over with and get on with my day. It felt like just a few strokes before my orgasm struck me. My mind rebelliously summoned the muscular arms and gorgeous ass of my new neighbor, and it sent me over the edge, my orgasm bubbling through me and emptying out onto the wet tile floor of the shower.

In the wake of it, I didn't feel that satisfaction one felt after good, hot sex; it was more of a hollow, fleeting relief I knew wouldn't last, but it was finished for the moment, which was what I wanted in the first place.

That urge now taken care of, I finished my shower, pausing to study myself in the long mirror hanging on the back of my bathroom door. I was of average height, around five feet eight, with skin that was still creamy and pale from the near-constant cloud cover of Seattle. That paleness was a testament to just how infrequently I'd ventured outside; was it even possible to live in Hawaii without being tan? I was living, breathing proof that it was.

A sparse smattering of freckles spanned out across my shoulders and the bridge of my nose. My body was normal, leaning toward skinny. I had a decent amount of muscle definition in my chest beneath a soft fan of dark chest hair. My stomach was just flat, maybe a bit soft. I gave it a little poke, frowning at just how flabby it felt.

There wasn't much I could do about the stomach, though, I thought as I toweled my bland brown hair. It was just shaggy enough to occasionally be annoying but wouldn't earn me the "surfer brah" stereotype.

I dressed in basic cargo shorts and a sky-blue polo shirt that brought out the flecks of blue in my otherwise green eyes. I'd learned to dress to draw out the few things I saw as my good features a long time ago, and my eyes were definitely at the top of that—very short—list. I didn't bother spending much time trying to tame my hair; it would simply do what it wanted no matter how long I tried to coax it into some semblance of order. I'd long ago given up that particular fight.

Dressed and ready to face the day, I set out to meet Grace. As I climbed behind the wheel, I was surprised to find that I was actually excited for lunch.

Chapter Two

I WAS NOT surprised to find Grace already at the restaurant. She sat in a booth near the back, facing the door, things spread out across the table that I was betting were not menus. When I reached the table, I wrinkled my nose in disgust. "Grace, this is a restaurant!"

She skewered me with her gaze, something that she managed to do in a way that no one else I'd ever met could master. Just that simple look from her could make a person feel like they'd said the dumbest thing in the history of mankind. "How observant of you, Gabe. Maybe I'm not the one who should be working as a private investigator."

"Since you know that already, maybe you can understand why it's a bad idea for you to have pictures of dogs taking a dump spread out all over the table!" I slid into the booth and collected the photos. She had twenty-three pictures of nine different dogs and their owners. The worst thing was they were high resolution. I placed the photos in a manila folder she brought with her. She reluctantly put it in the bag next to her on the booth seat.

"Have you been waiting long?"

"Not really. Maybe five minutes. I'm glad you decided to come out. It's about damn time."

"I think you're right about that," I agreed. The waiter came over and took our drink orders—a Coca Cola for me, a water with lemon for Grace—and vanished. "What are you going to get?" I studied the menu, seeing a lot of options with Spam in them, which I immediately ruled out.

"Probably just a salad," she replied. "I need to lose some weight."

I stared at her like she'd grown a second head. Not for the first time, I wondered if she had a mirror at home. Grace was utterly gorgeous, of mixed Islander and Korean descent, her facial features revealing both in well-proportioned ways. Her skin, already dark from her Islander blood, was tanned from spending all of her free time on a surfboard or in the water. The same outdoor activities kept her figure in great condition. The very idea that she could be fat was ridiculous.

I knew better than to say anything, though.

Grace flagged down the waiter, and when he came, she ordered for both of us. "Two mai tais and two loco moco, please."

"Maybe I don't want loco moco, Grace. Did you ever think of that?" I actually did want the loco moco—I'd heard a lot about it ever since Grace moved to Hawaii after college—but I wanted to give her a little hell. I didn't like when people ordered for me. It was something that Trevor did constantly, like I was incapable of making my own decisions.

"Everyone wants loco moco. Also, now that you're out and about again, we need to get down to the beach and get you on a board." A light kindled in Grace's eyes any time she talked about surfing. She'd developed the passion for it in college after she was introduced to it by some guy or another she'd dated. The relationship had lasted no more than a month, but it left her with a passion that would without a doubt last for the rest of her life.

"Grace, I don't know how to surf," I reminded her. "It wasn't on my list of things to do in Seattle. Trevor didn't really like the beach."

Grace's face darkened at my mention of my ex. "Of course he didn't. He couldn't make you spend ungodly amounts of money on him at the beach."

I conceded her point with a nod but didn't say anything. I didn't want to get into the Trevor talk right then, and certainly not with Grace. She told me from the beginning that my relationship with Trevor was a bad idea, and I didn't listen to her. I felt like she couldn't see the whole picture of our relationship, being so far away in Hawaii and only seeing him over Skype. It turned out *I* was the one who didn't see the whole picture.

Grace was a good friend, but she couldn't say no to an "I told you so" moment if it killed her.

Thankfully, Grace changed the subject. "Do you want to learn to surf? I could teach you."

"I hope this doesn't offend you, but I find the idea terrifying." I bore the middle finger she tossed my way with aplomb and dignity as the waiter returned with our mai tais. I sipped happily at my drink. "Are you sure these are such a good idea? I drove here."

"Come on, Gabe, it's just one mai tai. And if it makes you feel any better, I'll drive you around today and bring you back to pick up your car when we're done tearing up Honolulu. That way you can drink as many as you want until much later. Happy?"

In response, I took a nice, long draw from my mai tai.

We chitchatted about nothing as we waited for the food—Grace regaling me with the story of a client who literally jumped out of a second-story window after realizing he was being photographed having an affair.

"Dumb ass landed in the shallow end of the pool," Grace said, laughing. "He broke his ankle and then had to wait there, naked, for the ambulance because the lady he was having an affair with was too embarrassed to come out and give him clothes."

I couldn't help but chuckle too, even though part of me felt bad about laughing at someone else's misfortune. Then again, this one was self-inflicted, so I didn't think karma would come after me. "Did he think about just closing the curtains? There's something wrong with people who just have sex in clear view of their neighbors."

"I almost filed a claim for mental health services. It was bad. Thank you," she added to the waiter as he brought the two big plates of loco moco to our table. Loco moco was a dish made with rice, a hamburger, and topped off with an egg and gravy, and it was something I'd heard Grace rave about a hundred times before. It was time I tried it for myself.

"Oh my fucking god," I moaned after my first bite. It was such a simple thing, but it tasted heavenly. "How have I gone twenty-nine years without eating this?"

"You lived a hollow life before this moment," said Grace solemnly. "Welcome to true living. We're glad you've joined us."

I wasn't sure why I did it—looking back I could only say my inhibitions were lowered by delicious loco moco—but as we ate, I told Grace, "I met my neighbor today. His name was Maka."

"Ooh, an island boy, right? Nice. Was he hot? Don't bother lying. I can see your face—he's hot!"

Grace knew me too well to lie, and I didn't have much of a poker face, as she pointed out. "He was like a Hawaiian god. Literally the most beautiful human being on the planet, without a doubt."

"You've got to tap that—or get tapped, whichever one is most convenient," Grace insisted. "It is about time you get back on the man—

see what I did there? Instead of saying back on the horse I said back on the man because we're talking about sex?"

"Grace," I said, deadpan, "if you have to explain the joke, it isn't funny."

Grace huffed. "Says the guy who can't even tell a decent knock-knock joke. My point is it wouldn't hurt to get a little action, you know? Christen the new pad. You said he was your neighbor, right? Well, that makes a booty call really easy. No waiting."

"Shut up," I hissed, ducking my head down to hide my blush and forcing several forkfuls of loco moco into my mouth. Damn, but Grace had no filter, no matter where she might be. It didn't strike her as awkward to talk about the most intimate things in public, where other people were quite likely overhearing. "I'm pretty sure I won't be having a booty call with this guy. He's my neighbor, yes, but we talked for all of two minutes, and I don't even know if he's gay."

Grace made a *psshh* sound and said, dismissively, "Details."

"A pretty big one," I grumbled.

"I don't see why. Just *ask* him."

Grace made it sound so simple, but she didn't really understand the realities of being a gay man. I thought about Maka's almost bodybuilder-like muscles. That was definitely *not* the kind of guy you hit on if you aren't sure of his sexuality. I didn't know what it was, but something in the man's demeanor told me he definitely had the potential to be dangerous, and I could easily recognize that I had no desire to be on the receiving end of that.

Grace, though, was like a dog with a bone. Once she'd latched onto something it was damn near impossible to get her to drop it, and this would be no different, I could tell. "You can at least try to take him for a spin, you know."

"Can we just eat, please?" I pleaded, thinking I would die if my face got any redder. Had anyone ever died from blushing? I'd probably end up being the first.

"Okay, okay, I understand," Grace said, an amused smile on her face. I half expected her to keep heckling me, but she didn't, thankfully, and I finished my loco moco in peace.

"How do you eat that and still manage to move?" I asked when I'd taken the last bite. I felt like my stomach was going to explode and wanted to do nothing more than let myself sink into a blissful food coma.

"I guess you get used to it. Do you want another drink?"

I contemplated another mai tai, but decided against it. I felt myself edging closer and closer to a stupor after the meal and didn't think it would be smart to combine that with any more alcohol than I'd already had. Besides, it was the middle of the afternoon, and even after Trevor, I wasn't one for day drinking. I glanced at the empty glass at my right. At least not excessively. "I'm fine."

Grace waved down the waiter. "Check, please—all together," she added before he could ask.

"I can pay for myself, you know." I had never been comfortable with other people paying for me, even guys I was dating. My family drilled the idea that people should carry their own weight into my head at a young age—easy to say when you come from money. I'd managed to shake free of some of the more poisonous notions my father tried to instill in me, but this one had sunk in early, and it had a good grip.

"You don't have a job," she reminded me. "About that—I was thinking, why don't you come work at Paradise Investigations? We're always looking to expand, and you'd actually be making money instead of just living off your inheritance from your grandfather."

She had a good point, one I'd been thinking about myself. Hawaii was a really expensive place to live, and it wouldn't be long before my inheritance really started feeling the drain, even doing pretty much nothing every night and just staying in. It would be nice to have money coming in again, but being a PI?

"Don't you have to be licensed to do that?"

The waiter returned with our check, and Grace handed him her credit card, sending him off again. "Well, in an agency at least one person has to be licensed, yes, and we have two—me and my partner, Carrie Lange. You can get licensed yourself after working there for a certain period of time. It's kind of like an apprenticeship."

I almost laughed out loud at the idea of being Grace's apprentice. We loved each other dearly, thought of each other like family, but I didn't think that one of us having a position of authority over the other was a good idea.

We'd learned that when our sociology professor in college put us in the same group for a project. We'd both insisted we knew the best way of getting the project done, and neither of us was willing to compromise that. Our other group mates finally had to tell us to knock it off or they would kick us out of the group.

"What?" Grace demanded, catching my suppressed snort of laughter.

"Nothing, it's just…I don't think that I'm cut out for what you do."

Grace harrumphed. "We can't all be big-shot paralegals for massive Seattle law firms, Gabe."

The waiter returned with Grace's card and receipt, and we made our way to Grace's car—a Jeep Wrangler, of course, with the removable appendages. I could not think of a vehicle that better fit her personality. It was wild, meant for rough terrain, just like her. People took one look at Grace and thought she was just some dainty surfer girl, but really, she was much tougher than almost anybody I'd ever met.

I climbed into the car, buckling my seat belt as Grace got behind the wheel. "So, where are we off to on this magical Hawaiian adventure you're promising?"

"We're going to Waikiki Beach," she replied gleefully, turning the key. "If we're going to hit the beach, might as well hit one of the most famous first. We'll take the scenic route, and you can get a real look at Hawaii, better than the one you got in the middle of the night when I drove you from the airport."

"Sounds good," I said, settling back, rolling down my window to allow in the Hawaiian breeze.

"Will you put this on the floor between your legs?" Grace asked, offering me her purse. I took it, but didn't get a good grip on the second strap and it fell open, Grace's manila envelope sliding partly out.

Grace winced as she glanced at it. "We'll hit the beach right after I drop these off at work."

"So the first real place in Hawaii that you show me is going to be your office?"

"Don't look at me like that, Gabe, I have to get these to the office so they can be copied for our files and mailed off to the client tomorrow morning. I do have a job, you know."

I patted her arm comfortingly. "I'm kidding, girl. Besides, I want to see the place where your PI magic happens. I keep picturing it like it's in those old noir films—dark and moody, with all the lights turned off for some reason to show that you're a brooding investigator with a dark, heavy past that weighs on you and forces you into a bottle."

Grace laughed as she turned the Jeep onto the highway. "Wait, did you just call me an alcoholic?"

"If the wine cozy fits—Ow!" I rubbed my arm where she punched me ruefully. I forgot how hard Grace could punch. I would have to be careful not to tease her to that point too often, or I'd end up covered in bruises.

I sat back and got comfortable on the seat, listening to some pop song on the radio and staring out the window at the city as we drove through. It was amazing to see how different a city could feel depending on its location. Honolulu was not small, but it felt that way. Everything moved at a slower pace, everyone taking their time in pretty much every situation—the aloha way of life, or so I heard. In Seattle everyone felt so rushed, like there was no time to savor anything.

That was a big part of the problem with Trevor, too. Nothing was savored, even in our relationship. It seemed like we were just moving from one thing to the other, completing one stage in order to get to the next, not really enjoying where we were at that moment. Of course, that was probably because he didn't care for me at all, but still.

As I took in the palm trees and sun in the sky, I decided I could get used to the aloha way of life.

"We're almost there," Grace said, turning onto a street lined with businesses.

When she turned into the parking lot of a run-down strip mall, I was surprised, to say the least. From the looks of it, the shops had been abandoned for close to a decade; weeds were growing in the parking lot, and any signs of businesses had long since faded or been removed. Most of the windows and doors were boarded up.

"Did you make a wrong turn or something?" I asked, squirming on the seat. If it had been someone else's car I would have been afraid I was being led somewhere to be killed. Being Grace, this was probably some dumb joke of hers.

"No." Grace steered the car toward the far end of the strip. The very corner lot of the strip was still in use. It was a small space, probably once belonging to a Kinko's before FedEx bought them all out. A sign hung above the doorway, a simple one bearing the logo of a palm tree, its shadow, and the company name of Paradise Investigations. Below that was an announcement indicating they were licensed private investigators since 2014.

"*This* is your office?" I could not keep the surprise—and maybe a little disappointment—out of my voice. I didn't know what I expected, but hole-in-the-wall shop crammed into the corner of an abandoned shopping center wasn't it.

"What's wrong with it?" Grace asked defensively.

I paused, trying to find a way to be tactful about this; I knew how easily offended Grace could be at times. She was *not* a person who responded well to criticism. "I don't think people can see it from the street, for starters. Look around you—you're the last in a line of empty stores. People probably think this whole place is abandoned."

"We got what we could afford," Grace retorted frostily. "Not everyone has an inheritance to live on."

The barb stung, and I realized I'd offended her. A small wave of guilt washed through me. I should have been a more supportive friend. Could I really be that out of practice? "You're right. I'm sorry. I didn't mean to sound snooty. It really is awesome that you've got a place to call your own. Everyone starts somewhere, right?"

Grace pouted for a second or two more and then nodded, apparently satisfied with my apology. "Don't do it again. Let's go slip these inside. I'll give you the grand tour while we're in there. You can see what goes on behind the curtains of a PI's office firsthand."

"You mean it isn't anything like *Magnum, PI*?" I gasped mockingly. "If it's not, don't shatter the illusion, please!"

Grace muttered something under her breath and got out of the Jeep. When I got out, she was standing in front of the Jeep, staring at something. "What? What's wrong? Look, if you're waiting for me to make an admiring comment about the place, don't push your luck. You've heard all the nice things I—"

"Shut up, ass. The door is open." Grace pointed to the shop's front door, which was indeed hanging open, thrown wide by someone. It was one of those doors that was designed to close automatically, driven by weight, so it would have had to have been thrown open with a lot of force to break it that way.

"Maybe one of your coworkers is here?"

Grace looked around. "I guess so—there's Carrie's car over there." She pointed to a red Mini Cooper. "I don't know why she would leave the door open, though. Well, come on, you can meet my partner today, too. You're really lucky."

I followed Grace inside, looking around. I had to admire the décor, even if the place left something to be desired. Going through the door, a desk sat directly before me, an open door to its right. Beyond the door was a hallway of some sort, from the looks of it, but it was dark. Behind me and to the left was a small rack like you find filled with paperbacks at a book store, filled with brochures offering various services and describing the PI process. To my right was a long leather sofa—not one bought secondhand, either, judging by the great condition it was in.

Grace went straight for the open door next to the desk. "Carrie? You back here?" She flipped a light switch as she went through, illuminating the short hallway.

There were four doors, two on either side. The farthest door on the right was marked with a sign indicating the bathroom. The doors closest to me on either side had plaques, one with Grace's name, one with her partner's.

The door to Carrie's office stood ajar, though no light came from it. If she was in there, she had the light off. There was no way the office had a window, so that wouldn't make sense, unless she was taking a nap. Something about the situation put me on edge.

Grace walked to the door, rapping her knuckles against it three times. "Carrie? Is everything okay?" When no answer came, she pushed the door open, and stuck her hand inside, no doubt feeling along the wall for the switch. When the light came on, Grace let out a horrified gasp.

I hurried to her side, peering into the room. The state of it shocked me. Books lay scattered everywhere, a filing cabinet's drawers were pulled out and emptied onto the floor, as were the desk drawers. Somebody searched for something in there, and they left no stone unturned.

"What the hell?" I muttered, taking it all in. I didn't see it on my first scan of the room, but when my eyes swept by a second time they fell on what must have drawn such a reaction from Grace.

The leg of a woman, splayed out on the ground, disappearing behind the desk.

I crept slowly closer, heart pounding in my chest, roaring loud enough in my ears to drown out all other sounds. Bit by bit the woman's form came into sight over the edge of the desk. Sensible sneakers for the type of job she did, sturdy denim jeans, a button-down shirt, blonde hair falling over her face, coated with—

"Grace," I said, voice sounding thick and strange to my own ears, "call the police."

Chapter Three

GRACE NEVER WAS one to do what someone says without seeing for herself that there was a reason for it; why should this be any different? She came to stand next to me, starting to put her hands on the corner of the desk for leverage as she peered down, but I stopped her. A single shake of my head was enough to communicate my message of *don't touch anything*, which was good, because words didn't seem willing to come at the moment.

Carrie's prone form lay on its right side, and her hair covered the left side of her face, clinging to the skin and matted there by what looked to be a lot of blood congealing in her hair. Some also trickled down the back of her neck onto the floor. I felt like I was looking down on the scene through some sort of weird lens, a filter my brain created to separate me from the grim reality before me.

Grace let out a strange, half-swallowed cry and moved for Carrie, but I caught her in my arms. "Grace, Grace you can't," I said soothingly, holding her tighter as she struggled to get free. "You can't touch her or anything. We need to call the police; we need to get them here. Grace, *listen to me*!"

The sudden sharpness in my voice must have penetrated Grace's stricken mind. She stopped struggling, going limp in my arms instead. I carried her out to the front of the office, helping her sit down on the leather sofa.

"Listen to me, Grace, you've got to call the police, okay? I don't know the address to tell them."

It took a bit more coaxing, but Grace finally got herself together and placed the phone call. That done, she got up and started to pace, repeatedly running her hand through her hair.

"Who could have done this to her? Why? *Why*?" I knew the questions weren't for me, so I said nothing, just watched her, feeling numb, the filter still firmly in place. I had never seen something like that before.

Though I was no doctor, I had looked closely to see any signs that Carrie was breathing. Her back didn't move, nor did her hair flutter like it should have at any exhalations.

I'd just seen my first dead body, and the thought threatened to undo me. Now that Grace was taken care of, I felt myself racing toward that same mental cliff she'd stood on. What did one do in this situation? Other than call the cops, I mean? We'd done that, and now we were to wait there—but how could we possibly wait comfortably knowing what was in the other room? It was a form of psychological torture, almost.

"They were looking for something." Grace's pronouncement was loud and assured, drawing me back from that looming edge, just a little. "They destroyed the office because they were trying to find something."

I had to clear my throat several times before I could force words to come. "Makes sense, and explains the mess. But what would they have been looking for here?"

Somewhere in the distance, I heard the droning approach of police sirens.

The question gave Grace pause. "I don't know."

I sat down on the arm of the leather sofa, right leg tapping. I was aware of it, but completely unable to stop it; the nervous tic had been with me pretty much all of my life. The talking, the questions, it helped me keep my mind away from the back room, so I decided to keep it going.

"Did Carrie make any enemies? I mean, this job probably leaves a lot of people disgruntled, right?"

Grace snorted, the first indication of her typical mannerisms emerging through the haze. "I honestly can't think of a case that would lead to *this*." Grace gestured wildly toward the office behind them, a shudder running visibly through her. "The most disgruntled person I ever met came from a case we worked, trying to find out who was stealing food from a church food pantry. I don't think the seventy-three-year-old woman responsible held enough of a grudge to come after Carrie."

I fell silent then, unsure what else I could say. The flashing blue and red of the police sirens bathed the room through the window behind me, saving me the trouble of keeping Grace's mind—and my own—occupied. I stood and walked next to Grace, slipping an arm around her shoulder, squeezing to show my support.

A black sedan sped to a stop in front of the shop, followed by three patrol cars and an ambulance. I walked to the door to lead the cops inside and stopped short. I could feel my eyes bugging out of my head, but it was an appropriate reaction, considering the man climbing from behind the wheel of the car.

Maka.

My new neighbor was a cop. For some reason the sight of him struck me dumb. It made me feel somewhat better to see the same thing happen to him. We locked eyes, and he stumbled a bit, his own surprise clear in the small "O" his mouth made. He regained his composure faster than I did, though, probably because of his profession.

Maka's partner followed behind him. He was a beefy man, even beefier than Maka, though his girth was much less muscle and more beer, by the looks of it. He was a white guy, his hair dark brown and starting to gray. Unlike Maka he wore a suit, though it did not fit him well, and there was a stain on his shirt.

I recovered my wits as Maka reached the door, pulling it open and stepping aside for them to come in, followed by the other officers.

"What are you doing here?" Maka demanded as soon as he was through the door. His accusatory tone took me aback. He was angry at me for being here? We'd spoken for all of two minutes, and he was angry at me for showing up at a crime scene? I guess I could understand the surprise, but the anger was unexpected and left me confused.

"You know this guy?" Maka's partner asked, eyeing me suspiciously.

"No," I said just as Maka said "Yes."

"He's my neighbor," Maka said.

"But we just met today," I explained, ignoring the look of realization on Grace's face. "We only spoke for a minute."

The partner looked between us for a moment. "Let's try to keep it professional, yeah? I'm Detective Benet; this is Detective Kekoa. We're with Honolulu PD. We got a call from here about an incident of some sort."

"So why are you here?" Maka repeated. His tone still had the reproach from earlier that I couldn't figure out.

I bristled a bit. "Uh, my friend works here. That's why I'm here." I pointed to Grace. "She, I mean. She works here."

"Tell them about the body," Grace interrupted, her voice low, but teetering once more near the edge of hysterics.

It was a sobering reminder of why they were there. After that, Maka became all business. "Where?"

"In the first office on the left, through there. I'll show you."

"No," Benet interrupted. "You stay out here. I'm sure you contaminated the crime scene enough already. You can give your report to one of the uniformed officers."

Well. What a charming man. Sure, our inadvertent presence there, before we knew it was a crime scene, might have contaminated it a little, but I'd made sure neither Grace nor I touched anything.

Benet went into the back, Maka following behind him. Two EMTs hurried after them, one of them carrying what looked like a heavy duffel bag.

"That's your neighbor?" Grace asked when they were out of sight. "Jesus."

I didn't really feel like discussing him right then; it seemed unimportant, given the circumstances. Thankfully I didn't have to. The uniformed cops came up to us, leading Grace outside and me into one of the corners of the room far from the door, asking us to give a report of our day leading up to their arrival. The separation was probably to ensure that our stories matched without us overhearing what the other person said. I couldn't help worry about Grace's mental state at the moment.

The officer asking me questions was a young lady of Chinese descent, her hair long, pulled back into a ponytail that flowed out from beneath her hat. She had a small mole beneath her left eye that kept drawing my attention as she asked me questions, and I had to force myself to keep eye contact and not stare at it.

I walked her through the details of my day—minus the masturbating in the shower, because she really didn't need to know about that—at least three times, and each time she interrupted me to ask different questions.

"And what time did the moving company leave exactly?"

"Do you have the name of the movers that we can contact for verification?"

"Do you recall the name of your waiter?"

Things got really interesting when she started asking about Grace's partner.

"Did you ever meet Carrie Lange?"

I shook my head. "No. I've only been in town a short time and haven't met many people." I looked over to the door where a CSI team was dusting for fingerprints. "Uh, I touched that door to open it for the cops."

"We'll keep that in mind. I've just got a few more questions, please. Can you vouch for the whereabouts of your friend from this morning until the time you met?"

I blinked, confused. "My friend? You mean Grace? She was—that is, she had a case today. She told me she was staking out a lady's yard to get photographs. Why?"

"So you can't actually say with any certainty exactly where she was?"

Something in my stomach gave a queasy lurch. I didn't like where any of this seemed to be heading. "Listen, Officer, I don't know what you're implying—"

"I'm not implying anything, sir, I'm just asking questions."

The officer's calmness only served to irritate me more for some reason. "Well, your questions seem to be going down a specific path that I can tell you right now is ridiculous."

The officer didn't so much as blink. "What path would that be, sir?"

I opened my mouth and then closed it again. The officer was baiting me, trying to see what I was thinking—because if I could think it, then it couldn't be a far stretch. But I couldn't think it, so they were out of luck.

When the questioning finished, the officer told me to stay where I was, that the detectives would probably need me again. Grace joined me a few minutes later, looking exhausted.

"We call it in and get bombarded with insinuating questions," she grumbled, arms crossed over her chest, glowering at the collection of cops and investigators. "Should have just left it for Peter to find in the morning."

"Who's Peter?" I asked, more to distract her than because I cared. I couldn't bring myself to really care about anything.

"The secretary who works for us. We wouldn't even be here if I'd just managed to take the photos to Peter while he was still here, instead of going home before lunch."

I raised an eyebrow. "You went home before lunch? You didn't tell me that."

"Yeah, I wanted to change out of the clothes I'd been wearing in the hot car all day." Grace narrowed her eyes at me. "What's with that face?"

"What face? I don't have a face—this is just my...face." I looked away from her, feeling guilty for the brief flash of doubt. Grace didn't press the matter, though I didn't know if it was because she could see I was uncomfortable or because she didn't want to know what I might have been thinking.

As we waited impatiently the two EMTs emerged once again, talking in low voices, and went right out the door.

Grace watched their progress. "Why aren't they going to get a stretcher? They're driving off. Why didn't they take Carrie with them?"

I didn't say what I really wanted to: that obviously Carrie was already dead and had been since before we found her. It looked like Grace was barely holding on to her sanity as it was, and that might knock her off the precarious ledge.

Besides, she would find out soon enough.

Benet and Maka emerged from the offices ten minutes later, both of their faces grim.

Grace strode over to them, me right behind her. "What happened to her?"

"It looks like blunt force head trauma," said Maka, "but we'll have to wait for the coroner to know for sure."

Grace's had flew up to cover her mouth. "The...what do you mean the coroner?"

"She's dead," Benet said gruffly.

I glared at the brusque detective. "Your bedside manner could use a little work, you know."

Grace let out a strange sound, almost like air being let out of a balloon. And then, like that balloon, she deflated, leaning heavily against me. Despite what we saw in the office, she'd still held out hope that Carrie was alive, or didn't want to believe anything else was possible.

"She's...she's dead?"

"Yeah, she's dead. So we're going to need to ask you some questions. For starters, can you account for your whereabouts today?"

"I already answered that question with that officer over there." Grace pointed to the officer in question, a squat redheaded man who looked somehow out of place in his uniform.

Benet scowled. "Humor me."

We went through our day again, first Grace and then me, while Benet and Maka made notes. Every now and then, I caught a furtive glance from Maka, but he didn't say anything, and if I made eye contact he looked away quickly. What was going through his head? Was I a suspect? Was he trying to figure out if I was lying or not?

"Can you think of any enemies who might want to hurt Ms. Lange? Anyone who would hold a grudge?"

"I can't say Carrie was the nicest or most friendly person, but I wouldn't say she had enemies—not that I know of, anyway."

"What about angry exes or the like?"

"I don't know; Carrie used to say that she was a devoted spinster. I've never met an ex of hers." Grace trembled in my arms as they asked their questions. I felt bad for her, dealing with the weight of their interview, but it only made sense; I didn't know the victim at all, so could be no help in these questions.

"What about your relationship?" Benet inquired bluntly.

Grace glanced at me. "He and I? We're just friends—he's gay."

I barely stifled a groan at that. I couldn't believe she'd gone and said that, especially at a time like this.

Benet rolled his eyes impatiently. "I mean you and the deceased. You two get on all right?"

Grace stiffened in my arms. "What is that supposed to mean?"

"Well, isn't it obvious? You're her business partner."

Yup, definitely needs to work on his bedside manner.

"So that means what, exactly? That I killed her?"

"He's not saying that," Maka interjected tactfully. "But we do have to examine all avenues, I'm sure you understand. It's our job"

"What I'm saying," Benet growled, making a face in Maka's direction, "is that you could have some motive for wanting her dead."

"That's what I said, but I said it nicer."

Grace's eyes grew cold, and she stepped out of the circle of my arms as she leveled that icy look on Benet. "Carrie and I got along just fine, if you must know. Our business relationship was exactly what we both wanted—she handled business decisions, overhead and such, which gave me the free time I wanted. I just invested the money and got to put my name on the card, but she really ran the place. I was happy with the arrangement."

"Was she?"

Grace shrugged. "I imagine so, since it let her be the boss, which she liked."

"And did—"

"Listen," I interrupted, having had enough. "As I'm sure you can imagine, we've been through a lot, and we'd both like to get away from here. If you have any more questions I'm sure you can call us to ask them, right?"

Benet started to say something—a protest, I didn't doubt—but Maka spoke first. "That's fine, Mr. Maxfield." Benet's facial expression made it clear that it certainly wasn't fine as far as he was concerned. Something passed between them for a moment, a conversation that went unspoken. I wondered how long they'd been working together, to have a connection like that. They struck me as more like the odd couple, opposites who tolerated each other's presence but didn't really get along. Then again, I wasn't the greatest judge of people, so who knew.

"Write down your phone numbers and addresses in here," Benet grunted, shoving his notebook toward me. "And don't plan on running out, either. You should stick to the island until this investigation is concluded."

I rolled my eyes but said nothing, instead jotting my phone number down in the book beneath one of Benet's messily scrawled notes. His handwriting was terrible; I couldn't make out more than a few words on the page. When it came time to write my address I paused. I couldn't remember it off the top of my head yet.

"Don't worry about the address," Maka said, correctly interpreting my hesitation. "I know it. Since we're neighbors, I mean."

I chuckled at him despite everything, handing the notebook to Grace.

She took it with shaking hands, but her handwriting was clear and steady. When she finished, she shoved it back into Benet's hands as if she couldn't wait to get rid of it.

"Are we done here?"

"Yeah, we're done," Benet said dismissively. He looked toward the door as several people came in wearing dark blue jumpsuits marked *CORONER'S OFFICE* in yellow block letters. "Maka, the ME's here."

With a last lingering look in our direction, Maka joined Benet in conversation with the team from the coroner's office.

I grabbed Grace's arm and maneuvered her through the crowd of police officers until we were safely back at her Jeep. "Give me your keys."

"What?"

"Give me your keys. I'm not letting you drive home right now. I'll drive you to your place. Just tell me how to get there."

THE EVENING PASSED in a strange flux, seeming at times incredibly rushed and other times creepingly slow. It felt as if right after we reached Grace's apartment, the pizza we ordered for dinner arrived, and then it felt like we spent hours eating it. As we ate, we opened a cheap boxed wine and drank deeply from it.

Grace lived in a single-story duplex on a street filled with other duplexes. The living room was a narrow rectangle lined with a brown carpet. Her furniture fell onto the same autumnal color palette, from a darker green armchair to the burgundy sofa. The room had no overhead lights, instead several floor lamps cast their yellow glow about the room.

"I keep seeing her lying there," Grace said at one point. She clutched her wineglass in both hands as if it were a lifeline, the only thing keeping her from sinking beneath the waves of despair. Maybe it was. Her eyes stared off at nothing. We sat on her couch, the box of pizza half-eaten on the coffee table in front of us. "No matter what I do, I can't stop that image from flashing in my mind. It's like it was burned there. I don't think it will ever fade."

"It will," I comforted, though I honestly didn't know if I believed that myself. I knew what she meant; any time I closed my eyes the dead body of Grace's business partner flashed before my eyes as well.

"I've been trying to figure out why anyone would do something like that to her, and I might have something," she said uncertainly.

My ears perked up at that, but unfortunately so did my suspicions. At the office she'd said she couldn't think of anything. "Go on," I encouraged when I felt like she might not say anything.

"About two weeks ago, Carrie started going out of the office a lot. Much more than usual. I asked her about it, but all she told me was that she was working on a case—no details about it, just that she had one. Kept it real secretive."

"Is that strange?"

Grace took a deep drink from her wineglass before shaking her head. "Not really, I guess. We didn't always tell each other what we were working on, unless it was a two-man job. If either of us really wanted to know, we could just ask Peter or look at the files or invoices."

"Peter knew what was going on all the time?"

"Yeah. He handled the clients, usually, aside from our initial and final meetings. Also took care of billing, appointments, and filing, so he knew what was going on most of the time."

I started to take a drink and saw that my glass was empty. I considered refilling it—it would make for glass six? Seven? I couldn't remember—but I thought better of it. I already felt the blurry embrace of the wine clutching at me, and I didn't want to get any drunker—and I certainly didn't want a hangover the next day. For some reason, wine hit me harder than anything else when I had a hangover, the headache more persistent than you could imagine.

"I'm guessing you never said anything to Peter or checked out any of the files?"

She shook her head. "I didn't see a reason to. She works her cases; I work mine. That's how it works. Now, though..." She hesitated, brow furrowing. "Maybe if I'd known what she was working on I could have helped her in some way, and this wouldn't have happened."

I scooted forward on the couch, resting my hand on her shoulder. "It's useless to think like that, Grace. No one can say if it's true. It does you no good to beat yourself up about it." I cringed inwardly. The words didn't sound anywhere near as comforting as I'd hoped they would.

Grace took a deep breath—and another deep drink—and nodded. "You're right. God, there's so much I have to start thinking about. I have to make sure the business end of things stays in order." She laughed bitterly. "God knows I'm in over my head there."

"You'll figure it all out. I'll help you any way I can."

Grace threw her arms around me in a hug made awkward thanks to the angle we sat at on the couch and the wineglass in her hand. I hugged her back tightly, trying to say with that what I hadn't managed to properly say in words: *I'm right here with you, and I'm not going to let you go through this alone.*

"Okay," she said after a moment, pulling free of the hug. "I'm a little drunk, and there's a lot to do tomorrow. I should try to get some sleep." She rose to her feet, placing the wineglass on the table. She started to pick up the remnants of our dinner, but I brushed her hands away.

"I'll take care of that, it's okay. You just go get some rest."

For a moment it looked like Grace would cry, but she held herself together. "Thanks, Gabe." She hugged me once more and trudged off to her bedroom in the back. I tidied up the living room and put the wineglasses in the sink and the remaining pizza all into one box and that box into the refrigerator.

It wasn't until I finished that I realized my car was still parked in front of the restaurant we went to earlier. I couldn't go home, not until Grace drove me back to my car. It looked like I would be spending the night there.

I hoped the couch was comfortable.

I turned the lights off and padded over to the couch, lying down and finding a position to make myself comfortable. The couch wasn't making it easy, though. It was firm in places I wished were soft, and soft in places that were better firm.

I was in for a rough night.

When I did finally get to sleep, I had strange, shadowy dreams, full of prone figures whose faces I couldn't see, and loud, banging noises.

I jerked awake, blinking in the pale gray light that flooded into the room from the windows behind the sofa. That light placed it not long after dawn—the sky was still half-asleep, like me, but the sun's glow was slowly illuminating the world.

It took my sleep-dazed brain a moment to realize the banging from my dreams was real, coming from the front door. I lay there for a moment, perfectly still, hoping that whoever it was would go away eventually. They persisted, though, and I realized that anyone who was knocking on someone's door at the ass crack of dawn was probably *not* going to just leave.

I stood up, left hand clutching my neck and shoulder, where a crick had developed, and made my way to the door.

"Who the hell is that?" Grace said behind me. I glanced and saw her standing in the doorway to her bedroom, dressed in a tank top and boxer shorts. "Whoever they are, I hope they've made peace with their lives, because I'm going to kill—"

Grace stopped short when I opened the door to reveal Maka and Benet standing there, Benet's fist raised to knock again.

"Detectives," I said, not bothering to hide the annoyance in my voice. "Not that it's not nice to see you, but what the hell are you doing here?"

Maka looked regretful as he held up a folded piece of paper. "Sorry, Ms. Park, but I need you to step over here."

The blood drained from Grace's face as she did. Once she reached the door, Benet held up a pair of handcuffs. "Put your arms behind your back."

"What's going on?" I demanded as Grace complied. "Detective, what's going on?"

Maka didn't say anything, and Benet ignored me, addressing Grace. "Grace Park, you are under arrest for the murder of Carrie Lange."

Chapter Four

I STOOD THERE in complete shock as Benet read Grace her rights and started to pull her out of the apartment, stopping only when Maka suggested letting her put on some more appropriate clothes first.

My brain didn't seem to want to process what was happening in front of me; words were spoken, things were said—Maka attempted to speak to me, but I shook him off. The only thing I cemented in my mind was the number of Grace's attorney and her instructions to call him immediately and tell him what had happened.

I did that as soon as the police departed. God, it hurt to see Grace in the backseat of the car, being carted off to jail for murder, of all things. I don't know how the man on the phone understood a word that came out of my mouth; I had to be babbling, but somehow the message got through, and the lawyer assured me he would head right there.

I felt for a moment like I was going to shatter into a thousand tiny pieces. Everything seemed to be falling apart around me. I sat down on the couch, head in my hands, my nervous foot tapping, out of my control. I wanted to help Grace—she was my oldest friend in the world, and the only real connection I had in Hawaii. I couldn't imagine what she must be feeling. Was she scared? Was she angry? Did she feel alone wherever they took her? Were they questioning her right then? I wondered if interrogation tactics in reality are similar to what they show on television, the whole good cop, bad cop routine. Who was the good cop?

I thought of the regretful look on Maka's face. He didn't want to be there, that much had been clear. He was definitely the good cop. He'd even convinced Benet to undo the cuffs and let Grace put on clothes before they took her downtown, or whatever direction the police station was.

There must be something I could do to help, some way I could work to prove Grace innocent. I paced the floor of the small living room of her apartment, racking my brain to figure something out.

Of course! I stopped in my tracks, feeling as if a light bulb had just turned on above my head. Grace mentioned the case that Carrie was working on, the secretive one she knew nothing about. Grace was just grabbing at straws, sharing the first thoughts that came to mind, but couldn't she be right? Weren't the chances high that her death was connected to that case? If so, the files would hold the key to proving that Grace was innocent.

But how could I get access to those files? Grace's workplace would be surrounded by cops, a crime scene. No way I was getting in there. Even if I could somehow gain access, I had no idea what I was looking for, no way of knowing which of Carrie's cases Grace knew about and which she didn't, so no way of identifying the case that had put her life in danger.

The only viable choice, then, was the other person who would know the information. That would be that Peter guy who Grace mentioned, the secretary. She said he had access to all the files, so he would know something, if anyone did.

The kicker to all of that was that I had no way of getting in contact with this guy. All I knew was his first name, and I didn't imagine that would be the most helpful information. Part of me wanted to just sink into despair at that, let the obstacles overwhelm me, but I forced myself to stay calm. There was always an answer, if you thought about it, wasn't there? I mean, in the noir films the sleuth always came up with something when he kept his cool.

I wasn't expecting any revelations, but one actually came to me: I didn't know this guy, but Grace did.

When it came to being organized, Grace made it an art. She kept very careful, very organized notes from every single class we took together in university and filed them away, keeping them after the classes completed at the end of the semester. At the end of our four years of university, she still had the notes from our very first class. I wouldn't be surprised if she had notes from her high school classes stored away somewhere. I usually mocked Grace for this, calling her a packrat, but if I was right, I could use that organization to my advantage.

Somewhere in her apartment she had contact information for her coworkers, including this Peter guy. I just needed to find where she hid it. Given her organizational skills, I didn't think that would be a problem.

I started in the obvious place: Grace's bedroom. The majority of the space was actually devoted to work, as I expected. The full-size bed was pushed into a corner against the wall, a big desk occupying the majority of the room's space. The surface of the desk was neatly organized, the laptop in the center, a legal pad and pens for taking notes, and a Rolodex.

I snorted as I sat down at the desk and drew the Rolodex to me. This would be easier than I expected. Predictability was a wonderfully useful thing. I spun the Rolodex to the P cards and after a quick perusal found no Peter. Makes sense, I told myself. Peter was hardly going to be his last name, right?

That just meant I needed to flip through every card in the Rolodex until I came to Peter's and hope there was only one of him in here. Was it that common of a name in Hawaii?

The amount of names in Grace's Rolodex surprised me. She'd really been making contacts in her time in Hawaii. I guess I shouldn't have been surprised. Whatever Grace put her mind to she did well. Success was just part of Grace's makeup. I envied her that; I seemed to be the opposite, failing at every endeavor I attempted.

But this wasn't the time to get morose. There was a lot at stake here, and I needed to get moving quickly in order to find something that would prove Grace innocent of murder. Can't say I ever anticipated needing to do *that*.

I came to a Peter and pulled the card from the Rolodex. Just to make sure, I continued until I'd seen every card. This was the only Peter.

Taking a deep, hopeful breath, I called the number on the card.

It rang a few times before a groggy male voice answered. "Hello?"

"Hello, I'm sorry to call you so early. Is this Peter..." I glanced at the card to get his last name. "Peter Michaels?"

"It is." Caution was plain in his voice now, and I didn't blame him. I would be cautious, too, if I was receiving a phone call from a strange guy at the ass crack of dawn. "May I ask who's calling, and how you got this number?"

"My name is Gabe Maxfield—I'm a friend of Grace Park."

"I just heard about what happened to Carrie," Peter said, caution gone from his voice. "How is Grace doing?"

"Not good," I answered. "She needs your help."

After a quick explanation of what had gone down, Peter gave me his address and told me to meet him there so we could talk. I hung up and left Grace's house immediately. I had no choice but to take her Jeep, but

I didn't feel comfortable driving it all over Honolulu—and it didn't have a GPS system, which was a must for me and my level of familiarity with the area—so I drove back to the restaurant where my car still waited and left Grace's car there after calling a tow truck to take it back to Grace's place.

At a few minutes after nine, I brought my car to a stop in front of the house my GPS system told me belonged to Peter Michaels. It was small and cozy, with a beat-up green Mazda parked in the driveway. Looking up at the cozy place, I saw the curtains move and then flutter closed. Peter must have been standing in the window watching for me.

Before I even reached the door, Peter opened it, welcoming me inside. Peter looked to be fresh out of college, maybe twenty-four or twenty-five. He had large wire-rimmed glasses, a gangly body, all knees and elbows, and messy, dull-toned brown hair. He looked almost nervous to be talking to me, I noted, watching as he glanced either way out the door before closing it behind him.

"Right this way," he said, scurrying past me and leading me into a small living room off to the right. Spartanly decorated, the room felt larger than it was because of the lack of personal touches. A couch, a rug, a coffee table, a television, and a bookcase were the only things there. The walls were bare of pictures or art or anything that might give me some idea about Peter as a person. That in and of itself told me plenty.

I sat down on the couch toward one end, and Peter sat next to me, as far as he could be from me and still be on the couch. "Is it true? Did the police really arrest Grace for Carrie's murder?"

"They did. I'm not sure what evidence they have, but I hope you know as well as I do that Grace wouldn't do anything like that."

Peter nodded quickly. "Of course I don't think she did it. You said that maybe I would know something that could help her. What did you mean?"

"The best way to free Grace would be to figure out the reason Carrie was killed. Whoever did this also wrecked her office. Grace and I think they were looking for something. If they were, then it's likely that Carrie's death might be connected to a case she was working on."

"Paradise Investigations isn't exactly a dangerous work environment, Mr. Maxfield," Peter said with a high-pitched, nervous laugh. "I know television shows make private investigator work look glamorous and exciting, but from what I've gathered, the opposite is true."

"Doing your job, you would know a lot more about the cases that Grace and Carrie were working on, right?" I persisted. This was my biggest lead, the only real hope I had of helping my best friend in the world.

"I guess so." Peter squirmed uncomfortably. He was a jumpy guy. Then again, his boss had been murdered the previous day and now a total stranger was sitting in his house, asking him questions, so maybe the fidgeting was justified.

"Can you think of anything at all that might help? Was Carrie working on anything that could have led to this happening?"

Peter shook his head. "I doubt it."

I leaned forward a bit—not too much, because I didn't want to spook him, but close enough that he could see my sincerity. "Please, just think about it for a moment. Anything that can help, anything at all."

Peter sighed, pursing his lips, but I must have gotten through to him, because his brow furrowed in concentration for a moment. I felt a small seed of hope stirring in my chest. Surely this guy would know something, and I could take it to the police, and Grace would be out and they could go on looking for the real killers.

The hope died before it could take root. Peter shook his head again. "No, I'm sorry. None of their cases were dangerous or anything unusual for us. Although," he added, and the seed rumbled a bit in my chest once more. "It's always possible Carrie took on a case she didn't file with me. Sometimes they don't turn the files in until they've wrapped the case. But if that's the case, I can't tell you anything about it because I don't know."

I hung my head in defeat. I knew the disappointment I was showing would have been obvious to the thickest of people, but I couldn't help it. I'd really hoped that coming to Peter would provide me with something to go on, but it was a dead end.

"I'm really sorry," Peter said gently. "I want to help you; I really do. Grace is a great person and has always been kind and friendly to me. I just don't know anything."

"I understand," I said, doing my best to at least pretend to perk up. "It was worth a shot, right? And hey, if you think of anything, give me a call. You never know if something will spring to mind."

"I will, of course," said Peter, rising to his feet. Recognizing the obvious dismissal, I followed suit.

At the door, I extended my hand for a handshake. "Thank you so much for taking the time to see me so early in the morning, Mr. Michaels."

"Of course, Mr. Maxfield. I only wish I could have been more helpful for Grace."

I opened the door and gave a little start. For the second time that morning, I came face to face with Maka and Benet. Maka gave me a silly, unexpected half smile while Benet just scowled.

"Good morning, Detectives," I said as civilly as I could manage. I held my head high, ignoring the flutter in my stomach at Maka's smile and the closeness of his scent as I passed between the two of them on my way down from the porch.

"Mr. Maxfield," Benet called to me.

I grimaced and glanced back at him over my shoulder. "Yes, Detective?"

"What the hell are you doing here?"

I turned fully around at that, doing my best impersonation of my mother's patented stony gaze. "I fail to see how that's any business of yours."

Benet's face purpled, and he took a step off the porch. Maka stood behind him, looking nervous. "It's my business if you're interfering with a police investigation. That can be a pretty serious offense. I'd hate to see you end up in jail, too."

I rolled my eyes. "Spare me the intimidation attempts, Detective. I don't scare easily."

I turned on my heel and walked back to my car at a reasonable pace, all the while my heart thudded loudly in my ears. The entire walk I expected Benet to come up behind me and arrest me on the spot—not that giving lip to a police officer was a crime, but in this day and age, some police seemed to think not worshipping them was a crime. When I was safely inside my car, I looked back to the porch.

Peter looked even more distraught than he had when talking to me, and I couldn't blame him. I'm just an average Joe and a friend of someone he liked. These guys, though, they were cops. That would be enough to make anyone anxious.

I started the car and put it in drive, sparing one last look at the porch. At that moment, Maka glanced back over his shoulder. Our eyes met and a surge of lust rushed right to my cock. I really needed to get a handle on my returning libido.

I licked suddenly dry lips and pushed my foot down on the accelerator perhaps a bit faster than I normally would have, eager to put the detectives and the house behind me.

DRIVING HOME, I received a phone call from Grace's attorney, a Mr. Rembauer. He didn't seem too keen to talk to me when he did; I got the feeling the only reason we were speaking was that Grace insisted on it.

"Right now the police case against Ms. Park is thin," he informed me in his watery voice. When I heard him, I couldn't help thinking of a mole or a similar animal. "I can't tell you too much, as I'm sure you understand. I didn't want to tell you any of this, but my client insisted you be informed as much as possible."

I rolled my eyes, comfortable in the fact that he could not see me. "What led to her arrest in the first place? What could possibly make the police think she did this?"

Mr. Rembauer muttered to himself, no doubt wrestling with just how much he could—or wanted—to tell me. "They found her fingerprints on the murder weapon, a statuette from the victim's office. They were the only viable prints there. Combine that with the fact that there was no sign of a break-in and a series of rather terse text messages exchanged between them two days prior discovered on the victim's phone, and the police pegged that as motive." He huffed disdainfully. "As I said, their case is paper thin. It will not be too difficult to tear it to shreds in court."

The sudden intensity in the man's voice caught me off guard. I had been thinking that Grace would be better off with a better lawyer, one that looked like he could actually stand up and present his case in court, but now I reconsidered. Grace rarely did things for no reason, so something made her hire Rembauer.

As happy as I was that he was prepared to go to court and decimate the police case, I hoped to get Grace out of there before it came to that. "How soon before she has a bail hearing?"

"That will happen when she's arraigned. She was just arrested this morning, and processing will likely take some time, so I doubt we can make a docket before Monday."

I swore under my breath. "So she's stuck in prison—"

"She isn't in prison, Mr. Maxfield. She's in jail, or lockup, and it isn't anything terrible. She can survive the weekend. I will have her out first thing Monday morning—earlier, if at all possible."

Rembauer ended the call without saying anything more. I wondered for a moment if I'd be getting a bill for that call in the mail. More likely Grace would, and that was her problem.

EXHAUSTION DUG ITS claws into me pretty much as soon as I walked through the door of my condo. I refused to take in the boxes that were still there; I didn't have the energy to deal with them, and seeing them would just depress me.

I barely remembered entering my bedroom before I all but collapsed onto the bed. Sleep took me before my body struck the mattress.

Chapter Five

I STOOD ON a beautiful, white sand beach, staring out at an ocean bathed in moonlight. The moon hung in the sky, enormous and full. I could hear the waves, not a booming crash but a gentle slap as they climbed the sand, stopping short of wetting my toes.

"This is my favorite spot."

I jumped, surprised to find him standing to my left, staring out at the ocean. The glow of the moon gave his dusky Islander features an almost ethereal cast, like a statue that had been given life.

"Why is that?" If I sounded breathy when I asked, I chalked it up to our enchanting surroundings.

"Because there's no one around at this time," answered Maka with a mischievous grin. I had a moment to wonder about that grin before it became plain. Maka began to strip his shirt off, slowly revealing the muscled contours of his chest and stomach. I couldn't tear my eyes away from the sight; it captivated me in a way the ocean never could. My eyes traced the shirt's upward path, starting on the rocky plain of his abs and rising to the swell of his pecs, the dark nipples sharp points. The path continued up until our eyes met.

Something burned in Maka's eyes—something like triumph.

The shirt tossed aside, Maka's fingers dropped to the waistband of his board shorts, pushing below the elastic. He gave me a wink and then the shorts were down around his ankles, and he kicked them casually aside. My eyes did not follow the arc of the shorts; they were glued firmly to what hung between his legs, long and heavy, swaying like the pendulum of a grandfather clock.

"Have you ever been naked on a beach?"

"Uh…" Any ability I might have had to answer left me when he took a step closer to me. I thought it might be my imagination, but it looked like his manhood was thickening, perking up ever so slightly.

"It's probably the most freeing thing I've ever felt," he went on, voice becoming a purr, sex given tone. When his hands grasped the hem of my shirt, I could only stand there, entranced. The cool ocean air seemed to caress every inch of skin as Maka revealed it with the gentle touch of a familiar lover.

"You want to feel free, don't you?"

I nodded my head, heart pounding in my chest. At that moment what I wanted more than anything was to feel whatever Maka wanted to make me feel. Maka's hands grazed down my body to my own swim trunks, which were at that moment tented out by my almost painfully hard cock.

Maka saw my erection and grinned. He slid his hands lower, grasping the legs of my trunks. He looked into my eyes, never breaking contact, and jerked them down. My cock slapped loudly against my stomach as he released the shorts, letting them slide to the sand and allowing me to step out of them.

For the first time in my life, I stood naked on a beach, and I was with a man of godlike beauty—and godlike endowment, I saw, taking in the sight of his fully blood-engorged cock. Its weight made it too heavy to stand straight up, so it pointed out at a ninety-degree angle, like a compass arrow persistently pointed north.

"Isn't this amazing?" Maka murmured, stepping in close enough for our shoulders to brush as we stood there, side-by-side, naked and erect, facing the vast expanse of the ocean.

"Yes," I croaked. "Amazing."

Language abandoned me then, as Maka's hand enclosed around my cock, gripping it with a confidence that told me he'd definitely had practice on more than just his own. His touch was expert. He knew exactly when to tighten and when to release—when to expand his palm so that his flesh barely ghosted over my own.

"Feel me," he urged.

I didn't need to be told twice. I reached over with my left hand, encountering the hard-yet-soft flesh of his abdomen, which I groped for a moment before going south toward my goal. I wondered for a second if anyone had ever been burned by the heat radiating off a man's cock before. Maka's was hot to the touch, heavy in my hand. When I gripped it, my index finger and thumb could barely touch due to his girth.

I watched my hand sliding along his length, the foreskin covering the head before sliding back to reveal it, purple and leaking.

Maka moaned loudly. "Don't stop. Don't stop!"

I increased my pace on his cock, twisting my wrist a bit at the tip. Maka rocked back and forth on his heels, eyes closed, head thrown back as he abandoned himself to his pleasure—his hand still working my length.

With a guttural cry, Maka unloaded, spurting out onto the sand before us.

The sight and sound of Maka losing it spurred me closer and closer to my own orgasm. I could feel it building deep inside, my balls pulling in tighter, my shaft thickening in Maka's hand—

The rude, impatient blaring of a nearby car horn brought me out of the embrace of the dream. I lay on my own bed, panting heavily and coated with a sheen of sweat that had nothing to do with the temperature in the room. My cock strained in the confines of my underwear and khakis as I ground it into the bed beneath me with fervor. I was so close to coming, my release held back only by my self-control and desire not to literally jizz my pants. With great willpower, I forced my hips to still, arching my back so my cock was no longer pressing against the bed.

Once I drew back from the abyss, so to speak, I became aware of the room around me. It was dark; no sunlight came in through the window, just the pale glow of a light in the parking lot, a ways off from the window.

How long had I been asleep? I must have been more worn out than I had thought.

I rolled onto my back, staring up at the ceiling and trying to shake the final remnants of the dream. My cock refused to soften, though, despite my efforts, and that was only made worse by my realization that the literal man of my dreams might at that very moment be somewhere nearby.

Guilt gave me the power to resist my baser urges. The thought that while I was home, comfortable, Grace sat in a cell somewhere kept me from whipping out my cock and going to town. Someone had to help her, and there was nothing more her lawyer could do. That meant that responsibility fell to me.

I sat up on the bed with a sigh. What was my next move? Peter had been my one and only lead, and he'd given me nothing, dashing my hopes. But did he really give me nothing? Sure, he didn't have anything that he could tell me himself, but he did offer another avenue of investigation, which I would have realized at the time if I hadn't been so disappointed. I thought about the short conversation and everything he'd said.

Sometimes Carrie and Grace didn't file anything until the case was done. So what if whatever case got Carrie killed was one she hadn't finished? If that were the case, would she have kept her paperwork in the office? If so, then whoever attacked her probably took the evidence with them. But if not, the files might still be at her home.

But what if whoever attacked her had already been to her home, as well? It only made sense; they wouldn't stop at just searching her office, not if it was worth killing over. There wasn't much of a choice, though. I had to at least *try* to find something, even if I wasn't successful.

I turned the bedroom light on, not yet comfortable enough with this place to be wandering around in the darkness. My stomach growled; I hadn't eaten anything since pizza the previous night. But there was no time—I couldn't bring myself to eat, not while I could be doing something to help Grace.

I grabbed my keys and was halfway to my car before I realized I didn't have any idea where I was going. Oh, I knew my destination—Carrie's house—but where did she live? Cursing my stupidity, I went back into the house. The business card Grace had given me listed a phone number for herself and for Carrie, but that was it. No sign of a personal address.

Not knowing what else to do, I went to the computer and pulled up Google. I realized that I was an amateur, but if it worked for so many people, it was worth a shot. Much to my surprise, an address came up along with Carrie's private investigator's license. It was a matter of public record, and it looked like her home address was used. I personally would have never used my home address on anything of public record, but everyone had their own scale of what was safe and what was not, and I couldn't knock her for it.

Unless it meant that whoever did this had gotten to her house before me. That would pose a problem.

I wrote the address down and went straight out the door. Once I entered it into the GPS, it wasn't too difficult to make my way there— very few turns. It was nearly nine p.m. and the street was still full of cars. Was Honolulu ever quiet or calm?

At least I'm out and about. That's what Grace wanted. Though, I doubt she wanted it like this. Things were as they were, however, and bemoaning them didn't get anything done.

The GPS told me I was about four minutes out from Carrie's house, indicating a left turn up ahead. I soon found myself in an upscale neighborhood, where the houses sported nice big lawns, white picket fences, and porch swings. If I had to guess, I'd say Carrie's money didn't come from private investigating.

Carrie's home was inside a cul-de-sac with four other houses that looked exactly alike. I only knew which was hers based on the GPS. The house had no car parked in front of it, which didn't come as a surprise, since it was still parked in front of Paradise Investigations.

I started to pull the car into the driveway but stopped halfway through the turn. *What the hell am I thinking? What kind of idiot parks in front of a house that they're planning on breaking into?*

A cold sheen of sweat broke out on my forehead at the thought. It was the first time I'd actually given words to my intentions. I'd never so much as run a red light in my entire life, and now I was planning on committing a much larger crime by breaking into the house of a dead woman. If I got caught by the police, it would *not* look good.

Well then, I just won't get caught.

I backed out of the driveway and parked at the opening of the cul-de-sac, hoping that none of the neighbors had taken the opportunity to look out their windows and see me. It seemed like the sort of neighborhood that had a neighborhood watch, and I didn't need pesky neighbors coming to investigate, or worse, calling the cops.

"This is for Grace," I told myself firmly when I started to lose my nerve. She would do the same for me, in a heartbeat, so I could damn well do the same.

Double-checking the gloves I'd brought with me, I slipped out of the car and closed the door behind me as quietly as I could. I looked around for anyone taking out their garbage or venturing from their houses to pick up the object of a sudden craving or a late-night snack or even teenagers sneaking out to fuck their boyfriends or girlfriends, but saw no one. The cul-de-sac seemed eerily quiet and devoid of life.

With blood pounding in my ears and my breath so ragged I feared I might pass out, I made my way up the driveway to the wide porch of Carrie's house. I lifted the welcome mat but found nothing under it but dirt and a few ants. I felt around at the upper portion of the doorframe and also came up with nothing. I was hoping there would be a spare key somewhere—that way I could argue I didn't actually break and enter, only enter.

How else could I get into the house? Breaking down a door or a window would cause a lot of noise and risk disturbing her neighbors. It didn't help that I didn't know if I *could* break down a door; I'd never tried it before. It looked extremely painful, and I didn't much care to inflict pain on myself.

Maybe there would be an open window somewhere.

The sudden glow of headlights made me jump, and I turned around, just knowing I'd been caught, but they belonged to a car driving past the cul-de-sac. I doubted the driver had seen me, and even if he or she did, there was no way to know I didn't belong here.

Neighbors, though, they would know.

Feeling too exposed on the front porch, I started toward the side of the house. Near the front door was a garage, the door broken, like it had been knocked off its track and could not close all the way. The opening was wide enough that I could squeeze through, probably.

Was I really about to break into someone's house? I'd never even come close to breaking the law before, unless you counted speeding or accidentally taking gum from a grocery store when I was three—which my grandfather promptly made me go back and return, saying he was disappointed in me for taking it.

It's not like I'm breaking in to steal something—at least not for my own benefit, I reasoned. *I'm here to help out Grace.*

I got down on the ground face-first, the concrete of the driveway biting uncomfortably into my hands even through the gloves. Hoping I hadn't overestimated the opening, I crawled forward on my elbows, gritting my teeth against the discomfort.

The bottom of the door scraped against my shoulders, but I cleared the space without any real problems. I didn't want to look at my shirt and see the stains the door must have left behind; I just hoped they would come out. I really liked that shirt. Then again, that was my fault for wearing clothes I like to break into a house. I chalked it up to inexperience.

The garage was basically empty, save for a few piled up boxes, a rusty metal shelf with a few odds and ends for a car, and a lawnmower pushed into the corner. Not surprising; I doubted Carrie had much time or interest in the sorts of projects or hobbies people usually did in their garages.

I made my way to the garage entrance to the house. I tried the doorknob, not expecting anything to happen, and damn near fell into the house when the door swung inward.

Luck must be on my side tonight, I thought as I regained my balance. The thought was immediately followed by another: *I hope she doesn't have an alarm system activated.* No noise sounded as I made my way cautiously into the kitchen, and my worry abated some.

I used my phone screen to provide light, not wanting to risk the brightness of the flashlight or draw attention to the house. It would do. The kitchen looked fresh and updated—all of the appliances shiny silver, the countertops marble. An island stood in the middle with a built-in sink. I didn't think I would find anything of much use in there, so I made my way toward the next room.

The refrigerator caught my eye, and I could not help but stop. Magnets and pictures covered the silver surface—family portraits, Christmas cards featuring a woman who must be Carrie's sister, her husband, and two adorable children. There were coloring book pages torn out and added to the milieu, done by her niece or nephew, no doubt. The picture that kept drawing my eye was one taken at a beach. Carrie smiled out at me, clutching a surfboard beneath her arm. Her hair fell in wet tangles around her face. For a moment, my mind summoned the image of her lying on the floor, lifeless, bloody hair matted to her cheeks much like it was in the picture, and I had to look away.

A death like Carrie's would do that, sneak in and spoil the memories that were there, poisoning the past of the victim in the minds of those affected. If I could see one good thing in all of this, it was that Carrie's family didn't discover her. They might learn the details of what happened, but they would never see it, so the sight could not spoil their memory.

Get your head out of the clouds, Maxfield, I told myself firmly, stepping away from the refrigerator and its look into Carrie's life. *You're here to help Grace. Nothing can be done for Carrie now.*

The house was a single story, and the kitchen had two doorways. One opened out into the dining room, which itself led into the living room. The other, which I neared, joined a hallway leading away from the living room and toward the back of the house. The door directly across from me opened up into a nice bathroom, though I didn't stay to admire Carrie's decorating talent.

My stomach in knots, I walked slowly down the hall. Part of me still couldn't believe I was actually doing this, while another part did its level best to not think about it in order to maintain some level of control, otherwise I would curl up into a ball and have a panic attack, most likely.

The first door I came to was originally a guest bedroom in the layout, but Carrie had turned it into an office. It was a replica of her office at Paradise Investigations, I noticed; the layout was exactly the same, but with much nicer furniture. The wood looked to be expensive, the bookshelves one solid piece, not one of those assemble and slide in the shelves types.

The first thing I did was make note of the window on the wall. I needed to be careful to not shine the light in that direction or get too close to it, lest someone see me moving around inside and call the cops. The neighbors were bound to know about Carrie's death by now—it was in the papers, and I'd bet it made the news, too.

I started on the bookshelf directly across from the door, though it didn't seem promising. Quite a few technical manuals lined the shelves—I noted two guides to getting a private investigator's license in Hawaii, for instance—and books on a few other topics that didn't seem likely to shine a light on anything. The middle shelf had the fewest books, held in the center by bookends on either end. A small vase with obviously fake roses sat in one corner, while an old jewelry box sat on the other.

I moved to her desk next. The surface of it was immaculate, not a thing out of place. A Mac desktop computer sat there, turned off. Ignoring the computer, I tried each of the drawers. The top drawer contained paper clips, various writing utensils, a letter opener, and other stationery items. The second drawer, the bigger of the desk's two, didn't budge when I pulled. It had a lock.

I dug around the drawer above it in search of a key but found nothing. Figuring Carrie would be smarter than that, I started searching the second bookshelf behind me and came up empty again. Where the hell could the key be? She wouldn't take the key with her, would she, and risk losing it somewhere?

If it were me, I would put it somewhere I could access it when I needed to, but not risk misplacing. If the items inside were important, though, I would also put it somewhere a thief might not immediately look to find it.

I went back to the farther bookshelf and looked around it once more. After several frustrated minutes, my eyes fell on the jewelry box again. I took it from the shelf, placing my phone down in a way that the light would still illuminate the contents of the box when I opened it. The jewelry box was nothing special, a simple, oval shaped thing, the silver of it tarnished with age.

Inside I found a few odds and ends, and there—at the bottom beneath mostly useless things—was a small key, about the right size for a desk drawer. I scurried back to the desk. Anticipation had my hands shaking so badly that I missed the keyhole not once, not twice, but three times before I managed to slide it in home and give it a twist to the left.

I cautiously tugged at the desk drawer and it slid open. I bit my lip to hold back a cry of triumph as I peered inside. The inside was stacked high with papers, most of them bound and separated by manila envelopes. I dug them out, placing them on the desk and pawing through them. They were meticulously labeled—Paradise Investigations Bookkeeping 2013, 2014, 2015, and so on.

Just financial paperwork? I couldn't imagine how that would be any good to me. I highly doubted someone killed Carrie to get access to past bookkeeping records. I went through the envelopes one more time, dropping them into the desk drawer as I skimmed their label.

I almost didn't catch it—in fact, I only noticed because I happened to glance at the envelope one more time as I went to drop in the next one. Just like the other envelopes, this one was labeled Paradise Investigations Bookkeeping, but the year was for *next* year.

How could Carrie have access to bookkeeping for the future? It didn't make any sense. I tossed the others aside and picked the envelope up once more. This time I noticed the unusual shape at the bottom.

I lifted the brads holding the envelope closed and slid the contents out into my hand. Inside the envelope was a folder, the exterior labeled simply DELGADO. The strange shape at the bottom was from a film container, the sort of film that professionals used, the kind requiring a darkroom to develop.

This could be it, I realized. This envelope could contain everything I needed to get Grace out of jail. This might make the police drop their case against her so they could start looking for the real killer.

I couldn't wait to see Grace walk free, and I couldn't wait to see Benet's face when he saw how wrong he was and who it was that proved it.

Chapter Six

THE RETURN TRIP to my condo passed in a blur; I had no distinct memory of the time between leaving Carrie's house and walking back through my front door. It was probably a miracle I was alive. Thoughts raced through my head, the primary among them the desire to scour the documents now in my possession. I couldn't do anything with the film, since I had no clue how to go about developing it, but the police could handle that.

I turned on the lamp beside my couch and propped my feet up on my coffee table. With bated breath, I opened the envelope once more and slid the folder out, shaking the envelope until the film roll fell into my hand. I tossed the roll onto the coffee table, grunting in annoyance when it fell off and rolled to a stop in front of the entertainment center sporting my television. Whatever; I would pick it up later.

I focused all of my attention on the folder marked Delgado. That in and of itself was the first clue, I figured. Delgado sounded like a name to me—though first or last, I didn't know—which meant I had another suspect to put a name to, and that would go a long way to clearing Grace.

"No, Gabe," I told myself aloud, "don't get too far ahead of yourself. Right now, it's just a name." The last thing I wanted to do was move too quickly or make a mistake that could ruin my chances of helping Grace— or get me thrown in jail along with her.

Thinking of jail forced me to reflect uneasily on how I'd acquired this information. Would it even be admissible? Did the whole fruit of the forbidden tree thing apply just to the cops acquiring it, or would the fact I stole it make it useless? The question made me wish I was still working for a big law firm, so I could look through the law books and find some sort of precedent. But did the police *have* to know I'd stolen the material? I could always tell them I found it some other legal way.

Which would be perjury. Which could lead to jail time itself. Hawaii just kept getting better and better. Grace and I were going to have a long talk about this when I finally got her out.

I opened the folder and found myself facing page after page of handwritten notes. They looked to be in shorthand of some sort, and from the get-go, I could barely make out anything. The handwriting was slanted and full of loops and ornamentations that were absolutely unnecessary, and I wondered if Carrie always wrote like that or if she did it purposefully to conceal what she'd written, a sort of code of her own. If that were the case then whatever this was must have been really important—at least, I hoped it was, or it was back to square one.

I sat there for a little over an hour, staring at the indecipherable notes, praying that looking at the notes long enough would make the lines and squiggles make sense. That's how it worked in movies and on TV, after all: staring at the code long enough made something suddenly pop out and the entire puzzle fell together in fifteen seconds, flat. I had no such luck, though.

I leaned back with a groan, my neck twinging painfully. The notes were useless to me. I tossed them onto the coffee table and glanced at my phone, vision momentarily swimming. It was a quarter past midnight. It wouldn't hurt to take a break and get a shower, since I was making no headway anyway.

Left hand applying pressure to the crick in my neck, I shuffled tiredly back to my bedroom and started the shower running. I went to my dresser and dug out a fresh pair of underwear—boxer briefs, I liked the support when underwear hugged my body—and started back for the shower.

I'm not sure what made me stop, but as I passed the bedroom doorway, I paused. I heard a noise, a series of clicking, like metal pushing against metal. I strained my ears, trying to figure out where it came from when I heard the unmistakable sound of a doorknob turning.

But the front door is locked. I frowned, trying to make sense of what I was hearing. Was I hearing the neighbors coming home? I'd never been able to hear them twist their doorknob before—it made no sense now.

I stood there listening, thinking I'd just imagined the noise when a shadow moved across the floor of my living room. My blood turned to ice water in my veins. No doubt about it; there was someone in my house.

My throat felt tight and constricted and I struggled to breathe. Slowly, I stepped forward, hoping to keep my bare feet from making noise on the hardwood floor. My heart thundered so loudly in my chest

I was certain that whoever was inside could hear it. I cleared the small hallway in time to see a man, roughly six feet, clothed in all black with a ski mask pulled down over his face—despite the obscurity, I could see that he was white—standing in the middle of my living room, just in front of my couch.

The man clutched the files from Carrie's house in his hands.

There was no way in hell I was going to let someone take those, not after I worked so damn hard to get them in the first place. I'd broken into someone's house for those, for Christ's sake!

Instinct took over then. I rushed the man, despite the fact that he probably outweighed me by forty or fifty pounds. The only advantage I had was that he didn't notice me until I was basically on him. I jumped the last distance, knocking him backward. He maintained his balance, though, and immediately shoved me away. The back of my legs hit the coffee table, and I tripped, falling hard on my ass.

The intruder didn't concern himself with me after that; he made his way toward the door. I climbed to my feet and lunged, catching him around the middle and slamming him into the wall near the front door, hands scrambling for the papers in his hand.

The intruder's elbow slammed into the middle of my back, sending fire running through my nerve endings. My grip on his waist loosened. He maneuvered us around, using his body to ram me hard into the wall. The sound of my head slamming against it reverberated in my skull, and I released him, feeling dazed.

Before I could recover, the intruder slammed his fist into my gut, causing me to double over. For several agonizing moments, I thought I was going to throw up. I gritted my teeth against the pain and lunged forward, catching the man around the knees. He fell to the ground. I rolled to the side as he kicked out, striking the air where I had just been. His grip loosened on the file and I took my opportunity, jerking it from his grasp.

Now what? I had the papers, but the man's fallen body blocked my access to the front door, the only exit I had other than the small, enclosed veranda in my bedroom. I ran toward my bedroom, hearing the intruder getting to his feet behind me and swearing in a gruff voice.

I pushed my bedroom door closed, but before I could get it to click shut, the intruder's burly body slammed into it. It flew open, the edge of it striking me in the forehead. My vision swam for the second time that night and I stumbled back, falling into a pile of empty boxes that, at that moment, I really regretted not cleaning up. The rough edges of the cardboard dragged across the skin on my back and arms, and I would not be surprised if at least a few of the scratches drew blood.

The intruder stalked over to me, menace radiating from him in almost palpable waves. With every step he took, I could see my inevitable death approaching and knew there wasn't a damn thing I could do about it.

That didn't mean I was giving up without a fight.

I kicked out at the intruder as he stood over me, but my position gave my legs no strength; I might as well have been a toddler striking him. The man leaned forward, harsh blue eyes boring deep into mine. His left hand moved, grabbing my right wrist and jerking it around painfully until I dropped the papers. As he picked them up with his left hand, his right reached out, aiming right for my neck.

I struggled, raising my hands to deflect him, but he just bored forward, until his leather-gloved hand finally wrapped around my throat. As he began to apply pressure, I gripped his wrist, tugging desperately. My gaze was still locked on his, and as he slowly squeezed the life from me, his eyes showed nothing—no emotion, no pleasure, just a dullness that suggested this was not his first time doing this.

What number will I be? I wondered as I futilely tried to dislodge his hand. I had no idea what to do in this situation, how to fight him off. I thought about all the times Grace tried to get me to take self-defense classes with her in college, regretting telling her no. Hindsight was always twenty-twenty.

I thought of Grace sitting in lockup, alone and helpless. *What will happen to Grace?*

A knock on the front door startled my attacker enough that I could get my fingers down between his own and my throat. The knock came again, more insistent as I pried the fingers away from my throat, allowing precious air to flow into my lungs.

The front door opened then, followed by a voice. "Gabe? Are you in here?"

Maka! At the sound of the voice, my assailant leapt to his feet, and I coughed, trying to summon my voice.

"Back here," I croaked, doubtful that Maka could hear me.

If he didn't hear my words, he heard my coughing. "Gabe?"

My assailant looked around my room, spotting the small veranda door. He rushed to it, shoving the curtains aside and sliding the door open. He leapt over the railing outside and disappeared into the night just as Maka hurried into my bedroom. His eyes fell on me there, almost glowing with what I thought might be concern—and anger? Still unsure of my voice, I pointed to the veranda.

Maka hurried outside, looking around. He didn't see anything, though, because he came back inside, whipping his phone from his pocket as he did. "This is Detective Kekoa. I need police at my address. There's been a breaking and entry and assault."

Maka hung the phone up and stood over me, reaching a hand out to help me out of the box. I took it gratefully, not sure I had the strength to stand on my own. His touch was warm and comforting.

On my feet now, my legs were wobbly, and my knees quickly buckled. Maka caught me, pulling me against his chest for a moment. The man's body was like a heat rock, the warmth radiating off him and seeping into me. His scent swirled around me, cedar and cinnamon and male. I pulled away from him before my body started to react to his presence, taking a few shaky steps to sit down on the edge of my bed.

I still felt Maka's warmth, like a lingering touch, and flushed red despite the situation. I just prayed Maka didn't notice, or equated it with the struggle I'd just engaged in if he did.

"Want to tell me what just happened?"

"If I can speak," I replied, clinging to my sense of humor so I didn't break down in a nervous fit. My throat still hurt, like the man's hand still held tightly to it. My hand came up and massaged it, as if that could soothe away the pain. "What are you doing here?"

"I heard weird sounds and got worried. Who was that?"

"If I knew that, I'd tell you, but I don't."

"Well, what was he after?" Maka's words were short, like his patience was waning. "Or do you not know that, either?"

Well, I had to tell him eventually. This might not be the circumstances I would have preferred, but it was as good a time as any. I explained to him what I'd done—though I skirted around outright confessing to breaking and entering and stealing—and about the files I'd discovered.

"That's what the intruder was after," I finished. "This is proof that you've got the wrong person! Grace couldn't have done this; she's in prison!"

"Jail," Maka corrected, his face unreadable. "And this just proves she couldn't have done it *alone*. It doesn't eliminate her from being involved. She's got means, motive, and we haven't cleared her alibi yet."

"What motive could Grace possibly have?" I cried. I couldn't comprehend how anyone could think her capable of murder.

Maka studied me for a moment, and I could see the wheels turning in his head. He was probably wondering exactly how much he should tell me—if he told me anything at all. Finally, he sighed, running a hand through his hair. "A few days ago, Carrie accused her of stealing money from the company. We're looking into that, so it's not been proven yet, but it's still potential motive."

I couldn't believe what I was hearing. "So you think Grace killed her because she discovered Grace was stealing and then specifically took me to the crime scene?"

"It would make her look more innocent, being the one to discover the body—and not alone, either."

I knew Maka was just doing his job and thinking like a police officer should, but it infuriated me to no end. "So why don't you think I'm in on it?"

"We checked with your movers, and they were here, with you, at the time we estimate the murder took place," Maka said, showing the slightest hint of bemusement. "Besides, you couldn't have done it."

"Oh?" I crossed my arms over my chest. "Why not?"

"I don't think you're that kind of person," Maka said simply, the words stated with the utmost certainty in their accuracy. He truly didn't think I was the kind of person who could commit murder. I didn't know how to feel about that.

"You just met me yesterday, how do you know?"

The corner of Maka's lip quirked up. "Are you saying you want me to think you capable of murder?"

"No, but...just—oh, never mind."

"Tell me exactly what you found in the envelope," Maka said, reverting to business mode.

"A file marked Delgado, and a roll... Holy shit! A roll of film!"

I jumped off the bed, startling Maka as I rushed out into my living room. Where did it go? Had the intruder noticed it, too?

"What are you doing?" Maka asked, but I ignored him, eyes glued to the floor. Where had it gone? There! I reached down, snatching up the film roll. I brandished it victoriously at Maka.

"This!"

Maka squinted at it. "Film? Wait, this came from the file?"

"Yes! Whoever stole the papers didn't know pictures existed, I guess, or they were just in a hurry to get out of here. Either way, they left the film behind."

Maka reached to take it from me, but I put it behind my back and out of arm's reach. "That's evidence, Gabe."

"You can't do anything with it, right? It's fruit of the forbidden tree and all?"

A look came over Maka's face. "Why would it be fruit of the forbidden tree?"

Damn it. It looked like I'd said too much, and he knew it. The look on his face must have been his smug one. How could he even be beautiful when he was being smug?

"I...might not have had permission to borrow the file," I confessed, looking anywhere but at him.

"You stole it," he clarified. I nodded. I expected an explosion of anger, or even handcuffs, but instead Maka let out a chuckle, a deep sound that vibrated right to the core of my being. His expression was one of exasperated amusement. "That's a ballsy move, man. You're one crazy *haole*."

"You're not going to arrest me?" I couldn't help but ask. "Not that I want you to—I mean, I'd rather you didn't, but I'm shocked."

"I should, especially if it turns out to be useful evidence, but there are ways we can get it back. Let me think about it a bit. Until then, you can hold on to it. Pretend I don't know it exists."

I nodded, sliding the container into my pocket. There weren't words for just how relieved I felt.

The police arrived a few minutes later, questioning both Maka and me. Benet's arrival behind the police didn't surprise me at all, nor did the blatantly hostile attitude he took toward me.

"Tell me why you're suddenly the center of a lot of illegal activity the past few days?"

"Lay off, Benet. He was attacked," Maka scolded, earning himself a scowl.

"Okay, *why* was he attacked?"

"It's all in the report, brah. I'll fill you in on the details tomorrow."

Benet didn't say anything more, apparently accepting Maka's words, but the look he sent me spoke volumes. He did *not* like me. Well you know what? The feeling was mutual.

Just like that, I'd had enough. Not only was I attacked in my own home, but now I was getting the evil eye from some asshole detective? No thank you.

I stalked into my bedroom and started for my dresser. Maka followed behind me. "What are you doing?"

"What does it look like?" I snapped. "Getting some clothes and going to a hotel. Who knows how long this is going to take?"

"What if the intruder decides there's more they need to collect?" A furtive glance from Maka at my pocket told me what he was referring to. I was grateful for his discretion. I didn't expect him to conceal things from his partner for me. If I wasn't so worn out from the whole night, I'd have spent a little more time wondering just why it was he was willing to do so. "They found your apartment easily enough. What makes you think they won't find you in a hotel?"

"Well, I can't stay here," I said, exasperated. Why was this day just not cooperating?

"True. Your security needs a major update. Come next door. Stay with me till we get this figured out."

"What?" It was a good thing I couldn't see my own face, because I'm sure the look on it was bug-eyed and unappealing.

"It makes the most sense," he said with a shrug, like it was the most casual thing in the world for him to invite people involved in his cases to sleep in his apartment. For all I knew, it was. I couldn't help but think that would be a conflict of interest, though. "I can keep an eye on you, and you're close to home."

"Thanks for the offer, but I'll be fine."

"Consider it part of my duty," Maka's tone brooked no argument. "I'd like to keep an eye on my eyewitness and anything else that might be valuable." Another look toward my pocket, this one more pointed.

I realized I couldn't really argue with him on this, especially since he could easily arrest me. He had me by the balls, just not in a fun way.

"Fine," I grumbled. "Looks like we're having a sleepover."

Chapter Seven

MAKA'S CONDO HAD the same layout as mine, though he had much better taste in decor. I tried to tell myself that I had only just moved in and it would get better, but I knew it for a lie. You can lie to strangers, but you can't lie to yourself. I never had a real flare for decorating; my apartment in Seattle was Spartan.

Lamps in the living room cast a warm glow, and the kitchen area looked homey and used. There were pot holders and dish towels in a winery theme, and I noticed that the wallpaper was just bunches of grapes. The living room had a nice, comfy-looking sectional sofa in a chocolate color with red throw pillows added for color. Photographs hung on the walls, and I wanted to study them. A single low bookshelf lined the far wall, stuffed with books. Maka had framed and mounted his police academy certificate over it. The biggest feature of the living room was the massive television, at least sixty inches.

"Your place looks way better than mine," I commented.

"It's nothing special, but thanks."

When Maka walked past me, my eyes couldn't help but follow him, like they'd been caught in his gravity. He dropped his keys on a narrow table just before the door to the kitchen, and removed his gun belt. He hung it on a hook above the table—the holster strap unsecured, I noticed, for ease of access no doubt. He continued on into the kitchen before opening the refrigerator and bending over to peer into it.

Don't look at his ass, I instructed myself, even as my eyes went straight to the full curve of Maka's backside. *Okay, fine. Stop looking now, though.*

"You want a beer? After everything that happened, I'm sure you could use a drink." Maka looked at me from over his shoulder, and I snapped my eyes up to his, praying he didn't notice me oogling his ass. The last thing I needed was to make an enemy out of Maka, the one person other than Grace who seems to be on my side at the moment.

"Now that you mention it, yes. I would love a beer."

Not wanting to get caught staring again, I forced my attention to the living room, giving in to my earlier desire to examine the pictures he had around. The first few I came to, clustered together near the television, were of him and his family when he was young. In one of them, he couldn't have been older than four, and he was damn adorable, smiling this huge, carefree grin and covered head to toe in dirt. The woman with him, beautiful but ethereal-looking compared to the solid realness of Maka, held him in her arms, her own smile on her face, while a baby of one or two sat in the dirt, having the time of her life.

The second picture in the cluster featured an eleven- or twelve-year-old Maka, a boy already growing into the beefy body he had today. He wore a wet suit and had a surfboard held up over his head. Beside him, slightly in the shadow of the board, stood a girl who looked to be his younger sister, dressed in normal beachwear, no surfboard in sight. She had a smile on her face, but there was something fragile about her.

The third picture had a fifteen- or sixteen-year-old Maka—quite a stud, even at that age, I saw—once again in a wet suit, no surfboard this time, and a gold medal around his neck. His sister had her arms around his neck, proudly embracing him while he held up his medal with one hand and hugged her with the other arm. Studying the picture closely, I saw that she was definitely weak. Her skin was pale and something in her eyes spoke of suppressed pain.

The last picture in that cluster caught my eye the most. Maka stood in it, wearing what I could only call a loincloth, bracelets on his wrist and neck, and flower leis on his neck and head. His body glowed with sweat, even in the picture, and he looked happy. It was the first picture I'd seen without his sister.

"That's me after a hula performance."

To my credit, I did not jump in surprise when Maka spoke next to me. I hadn't noticed his approach, having been so wrapped up in the pictures. For a moment I felt embarrassed, like I'd been caught peeking behind a curtain I shouldn't have, but Maka didn't look or sound upset so I figured it was fine. I took the beer he offered me gratefully. I chuckled at the bottle, which sported a blonde woman in a grass skirt and a lei and was aptly named Bikini Blonde.

"*Huli pau*," Maka said, clinking his can against mine.

It wasn't hard to figure out what it meant, given the context, so I said it back, certain I tripped over the sounds somehow. "You look good," I said, gesturing toward the picture with the beer can. "The traditional uniform, I mean," I blurted when I realized what I said. "What is it called?"

Smooth. Really smooth, you idiot. Keep it up, maybe you can manage to make an even bigger ass of yourself.

"The loincloth is called a *malo*. The grass skirt is a *pa'u*—both men and women wear them, though the one worn by men isn't as ornate as the one worn by women. You know what a *lei* is, I'm sure. The bracelets, anklets, and headpiece are called *kupe'e*. Each dancer makes their own *kupe'e*, stringing flowers, beads, sometimes feathers, or even bones. It creates an experience unique to each dancer. The sounds or scents of the *kupe'e* draw the audience deeper into the hula performance. It is one of the longest-held traditions of Hawai'i."

I noted that there was something different about the way he said Hawaii and the way I did, a change in pronunciation that I couldn't quite put my thumb on. I decided not to try to mimic it; I would probably fail and embarrass myself and just show how much of an outsider I actually was.

"What brought you here?" Maka inquired suddenly, his too-intense eyes drawing me in. He sat down on the sectional sofa, patting the cushion next to him, like he wanted me to sit there. Before I could even register the thought, I sat down right next to him, even though there was a lot more couch I could have chosen.

"To Hawaii, you mean?"

"Well, I know what brings you to my place, so yes, Hawai'i."

I shifted uncomfortably, drumming my fingers against my beer can. "That's a bit of a long story."

Maka leaned forward, elbows on his knees and face turned in my direction. It looked like he sincerely wanted to hear the story, for some strange reason. "I'm sure there's a CliffsNotes version, right?"

I sighed deeply, not believing that I was about to delve once more into a pretty painful scenario, simply because Maka wanted to know. Taking a deep swig of beer for courage, I gathered my thoughts and strength to begin.

"I was born in Oregon, but went to university at the University of Washington. That's where I met Grace, on my first day on campus, actually. We became friends right away, not that either of us was surprised. It was almost like...fate, I guess. We were meant to randomly meet in front of the dorm. We asked each other for directions at the exact same time, and that was it. I know it seems silly and simplistic, but that's how our friendship started." I smiled wanly at the memory of the two of us, younger, both feeling lost and out of our element, standing there that late summer day.

"You know," said Maka thoughtfully, "most friendships we make in college don't last forever. That you and Grace are still friends, even though she's here and you weren't, that says something."

I thought about it for a moment. "I don't think it's possible for us *not* to be friends, at this point. I can't even imagine it, honestly. Anyway, back to my story. Junior year of college I met this guy—Trevor Berkley."

Maka snorted. "Sounds like a rich *haole* name."

"I don't really know what Howlie—"

"*Haole*," he corrected gently.

"—means, but you got the rich part right."

"*Haole* just means foreigner, someone who isn't a native Hawaiian—though usually it specifically means white people."

"So I'm a *haole*." It didn't sound negative to me, not exactly—at least not when Maka said it—but no one really liked being labeled as "other." "What if I was born Hawaii?"

"You'd be a local."

"But not Hawaiian."

"Right. Hawaiian is a race, you see, not something based on location. A white person born in Japan is not ethnically Japanese, right? The same principle applies."

I smiled at him. "Thanks for the linguistics and sociology lesson."

"Anytime." He patted my knee, his hand lingering. "Back to this *haole*, Trevor."

Trevor who? Maka's touch drew all of my attention, causing my brain to cease functioning properly as all of the blood began abandoning it for a more southern region of my body. Maybe Maka realized the brain-numbing effect he was having on me, or maybe he just decided it was time, but for whatever reason, he removed his hand. It took a moment, but brain function slowly returned.

"What was I...? Right, Trevor. So I met Trevor. He was the TA for a class on brief writing in corporate law I was taking—I majored in paralegal studies—and we kind of saw each other off and on for most of that year. He graduated at the end of it, though, and went back to Seattle, where he was from, and we ended things."

If only that was the end of his part in my story. Unfortunately for me, it wasn't.

"After graduation, Grace immediately flew off to Hawaii, and I started looking for good paralegal jobs. I happened to find one in Seattle and took it. I still had Trevor's contact information, so I told him I was in town, and he hit me up. We had dinner. One thing led to another, and within two months, we were living together."

Maka let out a low whistle. "That was pretty fast."

Hindsight was always perfect, and looking back, Maka was definitely right. "I didn't think much of it at the time, to be honest, and Trevor justified it by saying that we had been dating during junior year, so it wasn't all that fast."

"How long did you live together?"

I snorted bitterly. "Up until about two months before I moved here."

"So what happened to make you move across the continent and the ocean to escape?"

"How do you know I was escaping?"

The look Maka gave me could not have meant anything other than *Give me a break.* "It's not hard to see, if you know how to look. Everyone who's been hurt carries it around with them, in their eyes." Maka straightened, leaning toward me, too close, his eyes searching mine. When he spoke again, his breath ghosted across my cheek, and it was all I could do not to lick my suddenly dry lips. "Your eyes show it. He hurt you somehow, did something to make you run."

"Actually, he ran," I said, using my beer as an excuse to turn my head. "But it amounts to the same thing in the end, I guess. When we dated in college, he learned that I had a quite substantial inheritance left to me by my grandfather."

"I already don't like the sound of this," Maka muttered.

"Well, once we were living together, he started to say things like 'You can afford this more than I can' if we went out to eat or something, or if he found something he liked. If I brought up anything about going through the inheritance, he would remind me that I made good money, so we weren't living above our means."

"And what was he doing with *his* money? What did he contribute?"

"Unfortunately, that wasn't a question that crossed my mind. Which, of course, looking back, is quite dumb on my part. Things might have ended very differently if I had've asked that early on."

"What happened?"

"Well, I began to notice money going missing from my wallet and then from my bank account, in larger and larger amounts. I knew right away it was Trevor."

"How did he get access to your account? You didn't give him your PIN number or any stupid shit like that, did you?"

"No. We shared a MacBook. It was mine, but he was on it as much as I was. I was stupid and stored the passwords there, so he could log in whenever he wanted. I didn't even think about it at the time."

"Why didn't you call the police?"

"Because I loved him," I replied, surprised at the bitterness that could still seep into my voice, even after I thought I'd burnt away every last shred of any feelings, one way or another, toward the man. "I didn't want him to go to jail. I thought if I confronted him about it, let him know I knew, that it would stop and we could work on things."

"Are you always optimistic?" The teasing tone in Maka's voice right then was a welcome relief, allowing me to break up the heaviness I felt at that moment.

"Nope, just dumb." Maka's laughter empowered me, somehow, to carry on now that the hard part had been reached.

"I confronted him, and he got so angry—accused me of not trusting him, insisting that someone else had done it, that it couldn't have been him, if I loved him I'd never accuse him, things like that. He stormed out, saying he was going to go stay with his parents for the night, until I came to my senses.

"I felt bad, at first," I admitted, ashamed. "I should have trusted him more, I thought. What kind of guy doesn't trust his boyfriend? I tossed and turned all night, unable to sleep. All I wanted was to talk to him, to explain to him that I was sorry, clearly the money thing was just me overreacting, whatever it would take to make things right.

"I know," I added when Maka opened his mouth to say something, "it was stupid of me to feel that way. I see that quite clearly now. But back then...back then I blinded myself so much. I went out of my way to convince myself that I needed to keep Trevor, that what we had was real."

Maka patted my knee once more, and like before, he lingered there. Though this time he applied a gentle pressure. "Keep going."

"Okay. So, then morning came, and I received a phone call. My inheritance is kept in a special account, and I can only access the account once a month, and there's a limit on how much I can take out. It turned out Trevor tried to access the account to withdraw money, but couldn't. When that happened, he cleaned out my bank account and took just about everything from our apartment—which was in my name, as were all the bills, so he basically disappeared, leaving me with no money that I could get to."

I stopped there for a moment, not wanting to relive the rough time I spent in Seattle after that. Some memories were too personal, too painful to bring up.

"Long story short, Seattle reminded me too much of him and my own stupidity, and I wanted a clean break. Grace told me to come to Hawaii, since the break wouldn't get much cleaner than that, and I thought why the hell not. So here I am."

"You never called the police, did you?"

I shook my head, and Maka stood up, sighing like he was disappointed in me. "So the fucker just gets away with it."

I looked up at Maka, surprised by the vehemence in his voice. This wasn't even a situation that happened to him, and here he was, truly and visibly angry about it. It didn't make sense. "I don't see it that way," I explained slowly. "I see it as me freeing myself from him. If this had become a big thing, I'd be entwined with him for that much longer. As a police officer, you might not appreciate that, but I just wanted to put it— put him—behind me."

"So you're here in Hawai'i. Single, right? Ever been to an authentic lū'au?"

I blinked, surprised by the sudden change in mood and the new direction of our conversation. I'd have gotten whiplash if our conversation had been a road we were driving on. Single? Luau? *Single*? "Uh. What?"

"A lū'au," Maka repeated, like it was the most casual thing in the world, like he hadn't just completely jumped ship from the last conversation. You've seen them on TV, I'm sure."

"Yes. I mean, I know what they are. No, I've never been to one."

Maka grinned widely. "We'll have to fix that. Can't really say you live here until you've been to one. I'll take you to one soon."

Was I drunk? Had the beer hit me harder than I thought while I told the story? I checked my can—nope, still half-full. This definitely wasn't an alcohol thing, then. So what was it? There had to be an angle there somewhere, and I would find it. But how did I respond until I figured that out?

I went with a safe one. "Oh, okay."

Maka beamed at me. "Awesome! I'll find a good one to take you to. In the meantime, it's probably time we got some sleep. I've got work in the morning, and you probably have a house to break into or something."

I rolled my eyes. "Har har. It's not like I go around breaking into houses in my free time. And I didn't break in, the door was unlocked. I walked in, uninvited."

"You can coat it in creative words all you want; you committed a crime."

"So what? Are you going to handcuff me now?" I held up my wrists together in front of him. "I'm right here."

Something hot and powerful blazed behind his eyes, so intense that I could have sworn I saw flames. His voice, when his answer came, had dropped a solid octave. "Maybe later."

I sat there in stunned silence, staring at the wall behind him as he disappeared from sight, only to return a moment later with what looked like a comfortable, soft pillow and a thin plaid blanket.

"This should get you through the night. If you get too cold, the thermostat is on the wall over there, same as in your apartment. See you in the morning. Good night."

"Good night," I muttered, mechanically going about the task of laying out the pillow and unfolding the blanket. Even after the light was turned off and I lay there staring up at the ceiling—so familiar and yet still foreign, since I was acutely aware I was not in my own apartment—all I could think about was the heat in his gaze and the downright sultry words *maybe later*.

I DON'T KNOW how, but I managed to sleep like a baby on Maka's couch. From the moment sleep took me until Maka gently woke me at half past six with a gentle nudge, I hadn't even budged. If I dreamt the night before, I didn't remember it. Given the recent state of my dreams where the detective was concerned, that might not have been a bad thing.

"Does your hair do that standing up all over your head thing every morning?" Maka asked as he leaned over the back of the couch, looking down at me. He seemed much too awake for a man who could have only gotten five hours of sleep, max. "It's kind of cute."

I snarled wordlessly at him as I sat up.

The snarl did nothing to deter his lighthearted bantering. "Not a morning person? I'm not surprised at all."

I resisted the urge to say something really biting, reminding myself that it was my morning self that would be talking, and once I woke up fully I'd be fine. I went to the bathroom and did my business and washed my hands, splashing cold water on my face at the end to speed the waking up process along.

When I returned to the living room, Maka was pulling on an Aloha-print button-down shirt, complete with a black background and tropical plants in various shades of green and blue, not to mention the garish parrots.

I couldn't hold back a small laugh, earning an annoyed scowl.

"What are you laughing at?"

I tried to stop laughing, but I couldn't. "The shirt. I didn't realize people actually wore those here. I thought they were for fat, sunburned tourists and old men. Never imagined you as the Hawaiian shirt type of guy."

The look of offense on Maka's face was nearly comical. It might have made me laugh harder if I didn't think that Maka might haul off and punch me "These shirts happen to have a long and honorable history! Maybe if you're lucky I'll teach some of it to you someday."

I made a sour face. "That's what happens if I'm lucky?"

Maka pretended not to hear me. "Unfortunately, I need to go to work. We're going to try to check your friend's alibi again."

Just like that, the laughter I couldn't stop a few moments before died away. "Again? How hard could it be?"

"Apparently Grace's client hurried off to a family function the day after Carrie Lange was murdered and didn't leave a number where she could be reached," Maka explained as he buckled his gun holster to his belt. "We're trying to track her down, but it's taking more time than we hoped it would."

"And until you do, Grace is in jail." I couldn't keep an accusing tone from slipping into my voice. No matter how nice Maka was to me, he was still part of the police, part of the people who put Grace in jail in the first place.

Maka frowned at my tone. "Look, I'm sorry about that, but I'm just doing my job. But I am. Sorry, I mean."

His sincerity got to me, and I felt my ability to blame him slip away. He literally saved my life the night before and was looking out for me now by letting me stay at his place, and, maybe most importantly, he didn't arrest me for breaking and entering, theft, or obstructing an investigation, and whatever other crime I might have committed that I was unaware of.

"You should go see her," Maka suggested. "I'm sure she'll want to see a friendly face."

"Is that your subtle way of telling me you don't want me in your apartment after you leave?" I teased, even though I thought it sounded like a good idea. I didn't know why I hadn't thought to do that myself. Too focused on getting her out of that place to think about going to see her there, I guess.

"You caught me." Maka winked cheekily, and then he looked me over from head to foot. "Okay, I guess you should have a shower first; your hair still hasn't settled down, and you look a little sweaty."

I made a face at him, but again he was right.

"Just lock the door before you leave, okay? I know you can't lock the deadbolt, but you can turn the lock here." He pointed to the twist on the inside of the front door.

"I know how doorknobs work, Detective," I snipped.

Maka made a wounded face. "You're really snarky in the morning. That's going to take some getting used to. Be safe. Call me if anything comes up."

"I don't have your number," I protested.

"It's in your phone under Stud."

I skipped over the ridiculousness of him putting his name in my phone under *Stud* and went for the more obvious "How did you get my phone open? It requires my thumbprint!"

Maka shrugged innocently. "You're very suggestible when you're asleep. I asked you to show me your thumb and you did."

My jaw worked up and down, but I couldn't make words come out. He'd taken advantage of my sleeping state to gain access to my phone? Wasn't that illegal? I couldn't be annoyed, though, as I was too busy admiring the sheer brilliance of the move.

Maka took the opportunity to make his exit. "Have a good day. And *call me if anything comes up*." He shut the door behind him with a snap before I could get my brain functioning properly again.

Chapter Eight

IT FELT STRANGE being in someone else's apartment, especially someone I didn't know very well, so I took a hurried shower and put on the clothes I'd brought from my place the night before. I ignored all of the hair products on the counter, wondering why exactly he had a need for so many different things; I'd always only ever relied on a hairbrush or a comb.

Locking the door behind me, I stepped out into the fresh, crisp morning air and set out to visit Grace.

It would be easy for one to lose track of time here, I thought as I took several deep breaths. The weather was always the same, without a huge variance, temperature-wise, it seemed. Grace always told me Hawaii had two real seasons, and winter was definitely not one of them.

It was an ungodly hour for me, and part of me was tempted to go right back to my bed and sleep for a few more hours, but just the thought of going back inside after the break-in the night before left my stomach feeling queasy. Would I ever feel safe there again? Could I sleep soundly knowing how easily someone picked the locks on the doors?

I shuddered, a dark shadow falling over me momentarily, despite the beautiful morning. I needed to push those thoughts away and direct my attention back where it belonged. When I made my way to my car, I purposefully avoided looking at my condo.

A quick Internet search told me that visiting hours wouldn't begin until nine, which gave me a little under two hours to kill. Before I could even think about how to go about doing it my stomach gave a mighty rumble, deciding for me. I was much hungrier than I could recall being in quite a while, the pizza from two nights ago being the last thing I'd stopped to eat.

My second Internet search of the morning was for an IHOP. I couldn't remember the last time I'd had pancakes, and just like that, I craved them.

As I devoured my IHOP pancakes—chocolate chip—I was able to, just for a moment, pretend that I wasn't involved in my own personal episode of a police procedural on CBS. For that brief time, I could just indulge in the happiness that was fluffy pancakes filled with melted chocolate and coated in the Canadian ambrosia that was syrup, choosing to ignore the fact the syrup quite likely did not come from Canada at all.

With my belly full, my mood lifted, and time sufficiently killed, I set out once more, following my car's GPS to find the place Grace was being held. It was a bit confusing, and I got turned around a few times, but I finally arrived at the Oahu Community Correctional Center. The building's size blew my mind. The facility spread out over sixteen acres of land and, I later learned, could house nearly a thousand inmates.

Which meant that somewhere in there, Grace was sharing meals, a bed, maybe even a cell with criminals—or accused criminals. Was she scared in there? I would have been, no doubt about it. I assumed they kept pretrial and convicted inmates separate, but not everyone awaiting trial was innocent like Grace.

The sooner I got her out of there, the better.

Signing in to see her was a process that took quite a bit of time, and it looked like everyone wanted to go see someone in jail on a Saturday. After what seemed like forever, we had all been given the normal instructions—don't give them anything and don't touch them—and were now sitting at a round metal table in an uncomfortable chair, waiting for the people we wanted to see to be brought in.

A buzzing sound rang out through the wide, cafeteria-esque room, and several doors on the far side of the room opened, allowing in a flood of people in orange jumpsuits. Some of them were shackled at the wrist and ankles, while some weren't.

I craned my neck anxiously, trying to catch sight of Grace in the crowd. All around me, people were standing up, waving their hands to draw someone's attention. I remained seated, hoping it would help me stand out to Grace. It must have worked, because suddenly someone in the crowd broke off toward my table. Grace.

She looked a bit haggard and worn, but otherwise fine, thank God.

"Orange is really your color," I said teasingly as she joined me.

"Don't be an ass; it doesn't suit you," Grace fired back, dropping into the uncomfortable chair.

"I think it suits me just fine." I propped my elbows on the table, leaning in to examine her closer. "How are you? And I mean really, don't just tell me you're fine."

"What do you want me to say? I'm not staying at a luxury spa." Grace ran a hand over her face, slouching a bit. "Considering everything, I'm fine. My lawyer hopes to have me out on bail soon. I'm on the docket for first thing Monday morning."

"Well, hopefully we can have you out of here sooner than that," I said. I explained what I'd discovered at Carrie's house and what happened afterward. "Do you know anything about this Delgado thing?"

Grace shook her head. "The only Delgado I know is a business owner here in Honolulu. I don't know why anyone would want her to investigate him, though. If someone *did* hire her to do that, it could be risky. He's a very wealthy and influential man here."

"Risky enough to get her killed?"

Grace shrugged. "I really don't know—but considering someone tried to kill you to get that file, I'd say yes. You know, you could try talking to the last clients that Grace met with the day that she died. As far as I was aware, she was going to be in a bunch of meetings."

"Do you know who these people are?"

"I know a few names, but none of their details. All of that stuff is in the main calendar..." she trailed off, shoulders falling, and I guessed she'd hit a snag in her own trail. "The main calendar is back at the office."

I groaned, lowering my head to the cold surface of the table. I wanted to bang my head on it, but I doubted the guards would appreciate it. "The office that is now a crime scene."

"Yeah, that's not working out in our favor."

I started to reach for Grace's hand across the table when one of the guards caught my eye. He gave his head a firm shake and I stopped, resting it on the table instead. "Listen to me, Grace, I don't care what I have to do to get you out of here, I'll do it. I know you'd do the same for me. I'll meet with these people, somehow. I don't care if I have to pay my entire inheritance to do it."

"Just be careful, Gabe. You already nearly died. I don't want you to get hurt."

I rolled my eyes dramatically at her. "You overreact too much, Grace. It was just a bit of choking—maybe the guy was into erotic asphyxiation, that's all."

Grace's withering look told me just what she thought of my attempt at levity.

We chatted for a few more minutes, but it seemed like no time had passed at all before the guards announced "Time's up!" and marched the inmates back through the doors.

As I exited the facility, I called Peter's number, hoping it wasn't too early.

"Hello?"

"Peter! Hi, this is Gabe Maxfield. We met—"

"I remember," Peter interrupted. For a moment, I didn't think he sounded happy to hear from me. When he spoke again, though, there was no trace of it, and I wondered if it was just my imagination. "What can I do for you?"

"I was wondering if we could meet at your work this morning. I have a few things I need to find out, and also some information to share with you about what might have led to Carrie's murder."

"Did you find something?" Peter's voice sharpened, my words piquing his interest.

"I think so, yes. The only way to make sure, though, is to get something from the Paradise Investigations office."

"How quickly can you get there?"

I wasn't sure, given my current location. "Hold on a sec." I let the GPS do the calculating. "Not taking traffic into consideration, looks like about twenty minutes."

"Okay, I'll meet you there. Drive safely."

Peter's sudden eagerness reminded me that I could not have been the only person who really wanted to find out what happened in that office. Carrie had been Peter's boss, as was Grace. I'd found the perfect ally in my hunt—I was sure of it.

Traffic in Honolulu was the third worst in the nation, from what I'd heard, and this morning it lived up to its reputation. It took me nearly an hour to reach the offices of Paradise Investigations.

Directly in front of the office was the small Mazda I had seen in Peter's driveway. He leaned against the driver's side door, arms crossed over his chest, looking around impatiently. His tense shoulders relaxed when he saw me pull up.

"Sorry," I said, getting out of the car. "Traffic was a nightmare."

He gave a humorless half smile. "Welcome to Honolulu. What was it you found out?"

I looked around. I felt foolish doing so—there clearly wasn't anyone nearby—but after being attacked by someone I figured myself entitled to be paranoid. "Is it okay to go into the office?"

Peter dug into his pocket, pulling out a set of keys. "The crime scene tape is still up, but the police aren't here anymore. They probably processed the place yesterday, so it should be fine."

I followed him to the door, waiting as he unlocked it. I didn't really like the idea of going back in there, even though I knew the body was long gone, having been carted off to the coroner's office for an autopsy, but the image of it lying in the corner of that office swam to the forefront of my mind. Only the fact that there was no other way to get the information I needed motivated me to step inside when Peter held the door open for me.

"What did you learn?" Peter asked, closing the door behind me. His movements became somewhat automatic, no doubt the routine he went through every day. He turned the lights on and then made his way to the small desk there in the waiting area, taking a seat behind it.

I told him about the file and the theft from my home.

"So they got everything?" Peter didn't bother hiding his disappointment.

"Not everything," I assured him. Peter's eyes snapped up to mine. "He only got the notes Carrie wrote. Whoever he was, he didn't know about the film, and he left it behind."

Peter's brow furrowed. "You still have it, then? That's excellent! Glad that it hasn't all been for nothing. Let's hope the photos are enough to find who did this and clear Grace's name."

I thought about Grace sitting there in that orange jumpsuit, looking haggard and worn. "It better be."

"So what did you want to see me about here?"

"I went to see Grace today, and she suggested I talk to some of the clients Carrie was supposed to meet with to find out something about her behavior or mindset and get an idea of what was going on. Grace doesn't have access to that information—"

"But I do," Peter finished. Before I'd even finished my first sentence, he'd already pulled open the long drawer in the middle of the desk and withdrawn a soft, black, leather-bound desk planner. The thing was so big the dates could be seen clearly from the International Space Station. "Thursday, Carrie had four different clients to meet, starting at nine in the morning, the last at five—obviously the last two she didn't make, but the first two she should have."

Peter scribbled down the names and addresses of the two clients who Carrie had been scheduled with and passed them to me. "Did you give this same information to the police?" I asked, reading the names on the paper. Victoria Reed and Sakura Ohashi. I idly wondered what they would want with a private investigator.

"Of course," Peter said, sounding reproachful, as if I suggested he'd done something illegal. "I don't know how much they've investigated, but they have the information, if they want it."

"Thank you so much for this, Peter." I pocketed the paper and started for the door.

"Wait, just a minute," Peter called, stepping around the desk after me. "About the film roll, what are you going to do with it?"

"I haven't really thought that far ahead yet, but I guess I'm going to need to find a way to get them developed and see where they take us."

"Let me know when you figure something out—or if you need any help in that department. I'm sure together we could get it done."

I smiled at his earnestness. "I'll do that. Don't worry. I'll definitely keep you updated. I'm sure Grace will really appreciate this, too."

Back in my car, I set myself for the first destination on the paper. It only made sense to start at the beginning and see how far she progressed through her day before going back to the office.

Victoria Reed was an upper-middle-class white woman who, apparently, looked to hire the firm in order to find out if the man she was having an affair with was having an affair on her. She couldn't answer any question I asked her about Carrie's behavior—didn't even remember her name. It could not have felt more like a waste of time if I'd just sat in a parking lot staring off into space for the length of time I'd spoke with Victoria Reed.

Hopefully the second client would be more helpful.

As I was en route to the Ohashi address, my cell phone rang. I glanced down and snorted. The ID read Stud. I thought Maka was joking when he said he'd filed his number under that.

"Hello?"

"Gabe, I was just calling to check in on you."

Strange. I couldn't understand his fascination with checking up on me. Granted, that behavior came in handy last night, but it was still a little unsettling. "Who is this? My caller ID says Stud, but I don't know any Studs, so I think I'm going to hang up now."

"Don't act like you don't think I'm a stud."

I hated myself at that moment for smiling, but I couldn't help it. There was something about Detective Maka Kekoa that reached me, and I had little power to resist. "No, I don't think you're a stud—because, one, I'm not a teenage girl in the nineties, and, two, you're not a horse."

"I mean, I've been compared to one before, in some ways."

I laughed out loud, one loud *ha* before I managed to swallow it back, but the damage was done.

"Hah! I got a laugh. I knew you think I'm funny."

"Is there a reason you called, or was it just to overcompensate verbally?"

"Oh, I'm not overcompensating. Want me to prove it?"

I thought about the vivid dream I had of Maka, his cock big and hard. *God, yes, yes I want you to prove it*. But that was a thought I kept locked away firmly in my mind. Aloud I said, "Please don't."

"Okay, your loss. I was calling to check in, see what you were doing."

"Checking out a few leads."

"Leads?" The playfulness evaporated from Maka's voice like mist in the heat of the sun. "You should *not* be tracking down any leads."

"Well, Grace had some great ideas, so I thought I'd check them out while you were busy running down her alibi or whatever it is you're doing."

"That's a terrible idea," Maka said flatly. I could imagine the furrowed brow of disapproval on his face.

"Going to see Grace was *your* idea."

"I didn't say follow along a breadcrumb trail that she lays out, did I?"

"She's not the witch from Hansel and Gretel, Maka."

"The witch didn't lay the crumbs; the kids did to find their way home."

I gripped the steering wheel tightly, staring at the radio, through which the phone call was currently playing thanks to my hands free mode. Was he *always* this frustrating? "I just talked to a Botox-filled upper-middle-class WASP. I think I'm only in danger of boredom."

"Be careful, please? The last thing I need in my life is another homicide to investigate."

"Considering I like my safety, I can do that."

"I'm starting to wonder," Maka muttered. He sounded as frustrated with me as I was with him. "Oh, by the way, you need to be back at your apartment by six tonight."

"What? Why?"

"Police business. Just be there, okay?"

"Okay, I'll be there."

I brought the call to an end as I reached the address for Sakura Ohashi that Peter had given me.

Sakura Ohashi was a middle-aged Japanese woman. Her gaze was distrustful when she spotted me standing on the other side of her door— I guess I couldn't blame her, since I was a strange white male.

"Excuse me, are you Mrs. Ohashi?"

"I am," she said hesitantly. "What is this about?"

Beyond Mrs. Ohashi, I saw a middle-aged man, hair well-groomed, a perfectly trimmed beard, still black with barely any flecks of gray. He stopped a few feet behind his wife, leveling a hard gaze at me over her shoulder.

"My name is Gabe Maxfield. I'm here because Thursday you met with Carrie Lange from Paradise Investigations, correct?"

"You tell her we won't pay!" Mr. Ohashi marched to the door, gently sweeping his wife aside with his arm. "She's crazy if she thinks she's getting money for that bullshit consultation!"

The anger surprised me. "That's actually what I wanted to talk to you about, sir. Can you tell me about the consultation, about Ms. Lange's behavior?"

"There was no consultation," Mr. Ohashi snapped. "She showed up, talked to us for ten minutes, and then got a message on her phone and ran off. She didn't even have time to ask us about why we wanted to hire her in the first place."

"I'm really sorry to hear that, Mr. Ohashi," I said, hoping I sounded sincere. "Did she offer up an excuse as to why she just ran off?"

"Nothing," he spat. "Just said she needed to collect something from her office, asked us to call and reschedule. I told her no way in hell. I told her if she left then, she could just forget about our business. She said, 'I'm sorry you feel that way' and ran out the door."

I wondered what she could have read on her phone that would make her act like that. If there was something, then the police would have found it, since they had her phone and had found the messages between Grace and Carrie. Maybe they had more reason than I knew to suspect Grace. Perhaps Maka and Benet withheld something when they were telling me why they arrested her.

But her lawyer would know, right? Then again, Rembauer wouldn't feel particularly inclined to disclose the information to me, no doubt. If there was more, Grace didn't tell me. Maybe whatever it was simply wasn't discovered by the cops.

"Can you tell me if she was upset when she left or scared or something similar?"

"I don't know. She left too fast to tell." Mr. Ohashi scowled. "I don't care if she was upset; she was unprofessional, and she won't be getting our money! You tell her that."

I opened my mouth to inform them I couldn't do that—nobody could, because she was dead—but stopped myself. What good would come of that? All it might do is upset these people. Or it would just be information they didn't want to hear because they didn't care. I'd heard what I needed to hear from them, hadn't I?

Now I just needed to find out what it was that sent Carrie rushing back to work. What was she intending to do there? The files on Delgado were at her house, so she wouldn't need to rush to the office for it. Or was there more to the file that she had at work? Was a component missing? If so, how important was it? One missing piece made the whole puzzle useless, and in this, it might be no different. If there *was* something at the office, it might have been the difference between finding Carrie's killer and failing miserably.

"Thank you for your time, Mr. and Mrs. Ohashi. I'm sorry things didn't go well for you in your consultation. I hope that your situation can be resolved to your liking. Have a good day."

There was still quite a bit of time before I needed to go back to my place to meet Maka, so I went to the local library to use the computer and looked up as much information as I could about Delgado.

Most of the stories I came across were fluff pieces, talking about good deeds the company was doing, or research grants they were donating to local schools. Sometimes, though, in smaller papers, there were articles about some of the more underhanded and shady things reporters accused Delgado of. Rumors about the family being tied to organized crime on the island, that sort of thing.

The public face versus the private truth? My mother used to say that she was wary of someone who seemed too good, because it most likely was a façade masking something more. I doubted the good works and philanthropy of Delgado and his family were what led to someone hiring Carrie to tail him, so maybe there was some truth to the crime syndicate rumors.

If so, that was bad news. Everybody knew you didn't screw with organized crime. Police had to approach the matter delicately, cautiously, so a civilian PI? What could she have possibly been thinking? She as good as signed her own death warrant.

A grim thought struck me: had I done the same, looking into all of this? I'd already had my place broken into, already had someone just a hairsbreadth away from killing me. Had I put my own life at risk trying to help Grace?

Chapter Nine

I ARRIVED BACK at my condo at ten to six to find Maka leaning on my door, looking like he didn't have a care in the world. He was no longer dressed in the Hawaiian shirt, but a dark blue button-down shirt tucked into a pair of well-fitting gray slacks, Birkenstocks, and a nice woven belt. His hair was combed back similar to how it was when I first met him.

"There's something wrong with you, you know that?" I told him, pulling my key out of my pocket.

Maka looked himself over. "What are you talking about? I look great."

"You do. The thing that's wrong with you is that this is what you wear after work, but you wear Hawaiian shirts to work."

"Aloha print," Maka corrected. "You *haole* just don't understand Hawai'ian sensibilities. Go inside; get ready. We're leaving in ten."

I stepped inside the condo. A sudden flashback swept through me, stopping me in my tracks. Right there, in that very living room, I wrestled with an intruder. The lock on my front door had not done its job. It had allowed a breach of security—a break of my safety and trust. I doubted I could ever sleep soundly with that lock again.

"I'll get this lock changed," Maka said, jiggling the offending object. "I'll have the same security system my apartment has installed. It's much better than this flimsy piece of shit."

"You don't have to do that, really." I made my way into my bedroom to change clothes.

"I know I don't need to, but I'm going to. And by that I mean I did already. The team will be by tomorrow to install it."

"You know, most people ask for permission before they make decisions regarding other people's property." I pulled out a pair of dark wash jeans and a teal polo shirt, holding one in either hand and examined them.

"That's a good color for you," Maka commented from right over my shoulder. I nearly jumped out of my skin, wheeling around and skittering back so hard I bumped into the same boxes I fell in the night before. "You really should clean those boxes up. They are like a beacon for cockroaches."

"Why are you in my bedroom?"

"Because we were talking?"

"Well, want to go out into the living room?"

"Why?"

I held up the clothes in my hands. "I'm about to change."

Maka held up his hands in a *so what?* gesture. "Your point?"

"So, my clothes are coming off."

"I don't mind." Maka's face made it clear that it was not an argument he understood.

In the interest of time, I turned my back on him and undressed, shucking off my shorts and T-shirt and shimmying into the new outfit as quickly as I could. When I turned around, buttoning my pants as I did, I swore I saw a smile on his face.

"Are you ready now? We've got a place to be."

"Where, exactly?" I asked, fixing the collar of my polo.

"It's a secret, so let's go." He left the bedroom and then stopped, glancing back at me once more. "I was right, the teal looks good. Now come on."

Maka led me out to his car, a blue Ford Fusion, spotless, the sort of look that cars got when they were often washed or tended to by their owners. Maka was a man who kept his car well cared for.

"So, where are we going?" I asked once I was inside and buckled up.

"I told you it's a secret. I promise you'll like it, though." Maka looked like he was really enjoying torturing me, so I decided to stop letting him see that he was getting to me.

"Well, wake me up when we get there," I said with an exaggerated yawn and stretch. "I'm tired."

I crossed my arms over my chest and closed my eyes. I told myself I was only imagining the weight of Maka's gaze. For a moment, the steady hum of the tires on the road, the gentle swaying of the car, the soft freeform jazz radio station that was playing so low in the background I barely noticed all conspired together to make me feel drowsy.

As I drifted in that semihaze of being not asleep but not quite awake, the Ohashi family came back to my mind, and I wondered what case they wanted to bring to Carrie.

Carrie!

I sat up suddenly, remembering. "Maka, can I ask a question?"

"I thought you were sleeping."

"I'm serious. I told you earlier that I was going to talk with some leads Grace gave me. Well, one of them was an appointment Carrie had before she died, the same day. She apparently left it abruptly, after getting a message on her phone, saying she needed to go back to her office."

"Okay," Maka said slowly, waiting for me to explain where I was going with this.

"Well, you checked her phone records, right? You saw her messages with Grace. Do you know what message she might have gotten before she went running back to the office? What could have made her do that?"

Apparently Maka bit his lower lip when he was thinking—his white teeth flashing out, gnawing at the supple flesh had my blood stirring like crazy. It had been a long time since I'd had any fun, but I didn't realize how bad it was. If this guy—albeit a gorgeous guy—doing something as simple as biting his lip got my motor revving, I was in desperate times.

"The only text messages we read from that day were from the company bank, talking about an automatic bank transfer. Unless she got some messages she deleted."

"Or her attacker deleted them," I said, a sinking feeling in my stomach. "Which means that's another possible clue gone."

"Or there was no clue to begin with, and she simply forgot something at the office." Maka didn't sound like he believed that any more than I did, but I guess he had to play devil's advocate.

I slumped down in the seat, squinting in the late evening sun. Maka reached across and flipped the passenger-side visor down, blocking the sun from my face. I looked to him, surprised. He'd noticed something as minor as that discomfort and set out to alleviate it. Why did he keep coming to my rescue? I didn't believe that guys like him existed outside of Shonda Rhimes television shows.

A guy could really fall for Maka Kekoa.

We rode in companionable silence after that. When we'd been driving for nearly forty-five minutes, I turned to Maka. "Where exactly are you taking me, Maka? If you weren't a police officer, I'd think you were taking me somewhere to kill me."

He shot me a dazzling grin in reply. "There are worse places to be murdered, right?"

From the way his smile set my heart aflutter, I think I agreed with him.

The road he turned down off the highway went along the coast, and the sunset glistening off the water was exactly the image of Hawaii that I saw on television. For the first time since I arrived, perhaps because I had been viewing it for so long through the haze of Trevor, I thought that this was a truly beautiful place.

It helped that I was riding next to a truly beautiful man.

We came to a stop in a big clearing packed with cars. There was a big wooden sign, lined with flowers, at the far side of the parking lot, with words burned into it. The one word I recognized was lūʻau. I looked at Maka in surprise. "You brought me to a luau?"

"Why are you so surprised? I told you I would."

"You said 'soon.' I didn't expect that to mean the next day."

"Do you *not* want to go in?"

"What? Of course I do! Let's go." I unbuckled my seat belt and threw the door open before he could change his mind.

"Excited?" asked Maka with a laugh.

"Yes! Ever since Grace moved here, she would tell me all about the luaus, and I always wanted to come to one. So yes, yes I am excited!"

Together we made our way along a path toward a large copse of trees. There was a big stage and tables sprawling out from it like at a dinner theater. Along the back and side of the table area were long tables laden down with food. Men and women in the outfits like Maka wore in his hula picture walked around the clearing sporting trays of drinks.

"There are a lot of lūʻau places here on the island," Maka said. "And yeah, a lot of them are really fun. This place, though, this is a private lūʻau—not open to just anyone."

As he said this, we drew up on another smaller arched trellis gate, this one with two big men dressed in normal clothing standing in front of it, holding clipboards. "Names?"

"Maka Kekoa and plus one." Maka pointed to his name on the list and the two men stepped back, allowing us through.

I looked at him with a grin as we passed through. "Getting your name on VIP lists, Detective Kekoa?"

"Perks of being me," he said, wiggling his eyebrows. "The owner of this place is actually a friend of mine from my surfing days."

"So, does everyone in Hawaii surf? Is that like a requirement for living here?" I teased.

"Not a requirement," Maka smiled, "but there are tax incentives."

We found a small table for two and sat down. Nearly every table was filling up fast. The stage remained empty, but there was a crackle of anticipation in the air, like something was imminent. I glanced at the stage several times, expecting someone to come out on it at any moment.

"Can I get you a drink?" A pretty Islander came to our table, smiling at Maka before looking me over. She had skin that was a similar shade to Maka's, her hair, long and luxurious, tied into a braid, flowers woven through it. She wasn't just pretty; she was stunning. "You brought a cute friend this time, I see, Maka. Way better than that grouchy *haole* you brought last time."

Maka rolled his eyes, snickering.

"Wait, who was the grouchy *haole* you brought last time?"

"Benet." Maka snickered harder, and I joined in. Grouchy definitely described Benet. It was good to know that Grace and I weren't the only ones who felt that way, too.

"So," the woman went on, cocking her head to one side, studying me. "Who's your plus one this time?"

"Leilani. This is my friend Gabe. Gabe, this is my cousin, Leilani."

"Like...your real cousin?" I asked. Realizing it might have been an offensive question, I added, "I only ask because Grace told me it's common to call people cousin—or older men and women uncle or auntie."

Leilani laughed, and I relaxed a bit, deciding she wasn't offended. "Real cousin. Maka's father is my mother's brother. How do you two know each other?"

Leilani's tone was knowing, something suggestive about the way she emphasized know, and Maka glared at her, though she seemed unfazed by it. That cleared up any questions I might have about whether or not Maka was out to his family.

"He's my neighbor," Maka said, a warning in his tone.

Seeing Maka put on the spot was kind of fun, so I decided to keep it going. "We met the day before yesterday. I'm also involved with a crime he's investigating. Oh, and I stayed at his apartment last night."

Leilani's eyes widened, and Maka kicked my shin gently under the table.

"It's not what you think," I continued, unable to hold in my smile as Maka tried to tell me to shut up with his eyes, "though he did watch me change."

"Oh really?" Leilani then said something quickly to Maka in what I assumed was Hawaiian. Judging by the exasperated look on his face, she was continuing the teasing.

"Can we get those drinks now, please?" Maka begged.

I took pity on him and put an end to his torment. "Yes, I'll definitely have a drink. What do you suggest?"

"Okolehao," Leilani said immediately.

"No," Maka said, shaking his head adamantly. "Leilani, no. 'a'ole, 'a'ole."

"What's okolehao?" I inquired, wondering why it got such a reaction from Maka.

"You don't need to worry about that," Maka assured me.

"It's traditional Hawaiian alcohol," explained Leilani, ignoring her cousin.

"Is it strong, then?" This I directed at Maka.

"It is here," he said cautiously. "I think maybe something a little lighter would be better."

I bristled a bit. "What, you think I can't handle strong alcohol?"

"I didn't say that."

He thinks I can't handle my drink, huh? Well, I'll show him. I turned to Leilani. "I'll have this okolehao thing."

Leilani grinned triumphantly. "And what about you, cuz?"

Maka shrugged his shoulders. "Fine, okolehao it is." When Leilani left to see to our drinks, Maka turned to me. "I'm just going to say that I totally reserve the right to say I told you so tomorrow."

"I can handle my alcohol," I said defensively, to which he just gave me a *you'll see* look. It made me wonder if I'd made a mistake with this stuff. Or was Maka teasing me? I didn't know him well enough to know what his brand of flirting looked like.

"Leilani seems like a fun girl," I observed, watching her as she wound through tables, talking to regulars, laughing and touching their shoulders or arms.

"Fun is definitely a good adjective for her," Maka said, shaking his head. "Sometimes *too* fun, if I'm honest. Though, that's my auntie and uncle's fault. They named her Leilani, and they treat her like it, too. It means 'lei of heaven' or 'royalty,'" he explained when I just looked back at him blankly. "Her parents definitely treat her like royalty, too. She gets whatever she wants, does whatever she wants, and doesn't ever really see the consequences of her actions." Based on his tone of voice, though, I guessed that Maka was just as guilty of indulging her; there was no judgment or reproach there, just a simple statement of fact.

"'Lei of heaven,' huh?" I turned back to Maka, intrigued by this new topic to explore. "What does your name mean?" Did my eyes deceive me, or did Maka actually look embarrassed by my question? It couldn't possibly be *that* bad, could it? "Come on, what does it mean?"

"Nothing," he replied evasively.

"Okay, that's fine." I leaned back in my chair nonchalantly. "I guess I can just ask Leilani when she comes back."

Maka narrowed his eyes at me. "You don't play fair, you know that?"

"I know," I said with triumphant glee. "So you're going to tell me?"

"Fine. My name means 'favorite one.' I was the second born, but my father really wanted a son, so that's the name he chose."

"What's your sister's name?" I asked. The expression on his face caught me by surprise. He looked away from me, down at his hands on the table. "I'm sorry, if I..." I trailed off as Leilani returned to our table, carrying what looked like two mason jars full of water. As soon as she placed the jar in front of me, though, I knew it was *not* water.

"Wow," I said, the fumes of the alcohol making my eyes tear up. *Nope, definitely not water.*

Maka raised his jar up, his eyes daring me. "*Huli pau!*"

Full of regrets, I lifted by glass and clinked it against Maka's, resigning myself to my fate. "*Huli pau.*" My stomach knotted in violent anticipation of the torture to come, but I wasn't going to turn around and embarrass myself now by chickening out. This was my fault, and I'd suffer the consequences like a man. At least on the outside. On the inside, though, I'd cry like a baby.

As my first drink of okolehao burned its path down my throat and into my stomach, the only thing I could think was that I could *feel* it there, inside me. Most drinks, you swallow them, they go down, and then you forget about them. Not this thing, though.

"This tastes like rubbing alcohol," I hissed, shuddering and reaching for a glass of water, which only helped a little bit.

"It's moonshine," Maka said, drinking from his as if it were actually water.

I narrowed my eyes suspiciously at him. "What are you drinking?"

"The same thing you are." Maka held his glass out for me to sniff, and I turned my head aside. "Leilani, why don't you bring us a pitcher of pineapple juice and two glasses?"

"Are we quitting?" I couldn't hide the hopefulness that crept into my voice.

"No, just trust me."

Leilani returned with the pineapple juice and glasses and Maka proceeded to pour the glasses two thirds full of pineapple juice and then added a third of the okolehao. "Okay," he said, shaking the glass to stir the concoction before passing it to me. "Try it now."

I sniffed tentatively at it. The pineapple juice certainly reduced the nose-hair burning smell of it. As for the taste, well nothing for that but to drink. I took a sip and then a bigger drink. "Oh! Wow, that's actually much better!"

The sun was basically gone now, and tiki torches had been lit along the perimeter and at various stages throughout the spread of tables. An MC, a large Islander man with a booming voice in no need of a microphone, came onto the stage and made an opening speech, but by that point, I was already viewing the world through the vapor haze of okolehao. I didn't realize it right away, and when I did I was surprised. How had it crept up on me so stealthily?

I eyed the mason jar. I'd have to tread carefully with this stuff.

After the speech, a roar of applause and cheers went up from the spectators, drawing my attention back to the stage as three men, bodies muscled and oiled, stepped out onto the stage, carrying something in their hands.

"I see your attention has returned," Maka said, mock-scathingly. "Though I definitely can't blame you."

"What are they about to do?" I asked.

"Just watch and see."

"But what are they—whoa!" A flash of fire on the stage interrupted me, as the three men, in unison, stuck whatever they were carrying into a torch near them, lighting the ends on fire. Drums began to play, a driving, rhythmic tone that spoke of history and ritual and the heartbeat of the planet. And the men danced.

It was powerful and enchanting, the fire leaving burning streaks in the air in its wake as they twirled and danced and moved their bodies. I couldn't look away; it was like their dance cast a spell over me—and not just me, I realized, but the whole crowd. A hush had fallen as conversations died down, every ounce of attention focused on the three men on stage.

When it ended, we in the audience let out collective breaths that I doubted anyone realized they'd been holding.

"They were fire dancers," Maka explained to me when the applause died down. His voice carried a tone of awe that surprised me a little. He'd probably seen that sort of thing a hundred times over in his life.

"They were awesome." I fumbled with the pitcher of pineapple juice, sloshing some on the table, and Maka took the pitcher from me.

"Before you drink more, we need to get some food in you, okay? There are buffet tables over there."

I made three attempts before I finally managed to get to my feet, using the table and the back of my chair for balance. Dizziness swept over me in waves, some worse than others. How was that even possible? I hadn't had that much to drink, had I?

I studied the table for some clue to my inebriation. I saw my mason jar was empty, and Maka's was getting there. And yet he seemed to be perfectly fine. How? Was he secretly Superman and I just hadn't caught on?

"Come on, Gabe." Maka slid one arm around my waist as he guided me through the throng of people to the tables laden down with food. I stumbled once, but Maka's arms held me up. "*Haole* are such lightweights."

"I'm not a lightweight," I protested, turning my head so he could see my glare. I needed, *needed* him to see my glare at that moment. "Look at it! Look at my glare."

"It's terrifying. Look." Maka gestured toward the buffet. "What do you want to eat?"

Everything on the tables looked delicious. I pointed things out to Maka as we went down the line, and he dished it out onto plates.

"Maka, howzit, brah?" I glanced around, trying to find the source of the words, and looked at the big MC. "Who's your *haole* friend?"

"He's talking about me," I informed Maka, in case he didn't realize. "I'm a *haole*."

"This is Gabe," Maka said, giving me a bemused look. "My neighbor."

"I slept at his place last night," I put in, trying to be helpful.

The MC tried to hide his smile, raising an eyebrow at Maka. "That so?"

"It's a long story, Hiapo. He's only been in Honolulu for a few weeks. Thought I'd show him the best *lū'au* on the island."

Hiapo clapped Maka's shoulder appreciatively at the compliment. "You picked the right one then, brah. So, *haole*, you ready for choke grindin'?" He eyed the plate Maka was carrying for me. "I'd say you are."

"Grinding?" My mind immediately went to a dirty place, and I imagined myself grinding hard against Maka's buff body. *What are you doing?* wondered the last sane voice in my head. It was that voice to which I normally listened, but tonight I was far too lost to the moonshine to care.

"He means eating," Maka hurriedly explained. Something in his heavy gaze told me Maka knew where my thoughts were. Something else—thought it could have been my imagination—told me he didn't disapprove.

"I got the best thing for yah, my *haole* brother. Come with me."

Hiapo threw his heavy arm around my shoulder, and I staggered, Maka again catching me. "Lemme guess, okolehao?"

At the mention of the potent alcohol, I perked up. "We should totally get more of that!"

"I'm pretty sure you've about had enough," Maka argued firmly.

"The man knows what he wants," Hiapo said firmly. "He wants okolehao, he gonna get okolehao."

"I like this guy," I informed Maka decisively. "He knows me."

Hiapo's booming laughter vibrated through my body, and I laughed too.

Maka finally led me back to our table, plates laden with food.

Hiapo made good on his promise, sending out another pitcher of pineapple juice and another mason jar of the drink that was my best friend for the rest of the night.

At some point throughout the festivities, a hula show began, with male dancers on the stage and female dancers working their way through the audience, along a 360-degree view of what the performance looked like instead of just a front-facing view.

Like the fire dance, I found myself mesmerized by the sway of the hips, the movement of the grass skirts—the *pa'u*—and the flickering torchlight reflecting off of the *kupe'e* on their wrists and ankles. If I could do that, if I could pull off those moves, then I would never stop dancing.

"Gabe, you're going to fall out of your chair," Maka said.

I wondered what he meant until I realized I was dancing in my chair. I stopped, embarrassed, and returned my focus to the dance. One of the dancers wound her way through the tables, coming close to ours. She smiled at Maka, beautifully dark-painted lips spreading to expose white teeth. She winked at him, tossing him the *lei* from around her neck, while the onlookers cheered.

It was a meaningless gesture—and an understandable one, because Maka was a stud, as he put it—but it set my blood boiling. I gripped the glass of pineapple juice and okolehao so tightly I thought my knuckles were going to burst through my skin. When she offered me a smile, I stuck my tongue out at her.

That would show her.

When the dance finished, Hiapo announced a grand unveiling. He called everyone to gather around a big circle off to the side, surrounded by more torches. The circle, I saw when I stood there looking down at it next to Maka, was made of sand.

"And now," Hiapo said loudly, "what everyone's been waiting for! Let's see it!"

At his words, two men in the fire dancer costumes came with shovels and began uncovering something in the center.

"What are they doing?" I asked Maka in a loud whisper. He just shushed me and pointed to the sand. They eventually uncovered what looked like a bamboo lid underneath a bunch of palm tree leaves. "What's in there?"

He didn't answer. Somewhere drums began beating a rapid tempo, though I guess I couldn't be sure it wasn't in my drunk imagination. The lid came off and delicious smelling smoke wafted up. The men hefted a long pole, and from the hole, they lifted what everyone had been waiting for.

"It's a pig!" I cried, pointing at it. "That poor pig!"

"It's dead, Gabe," Maka assured me, not bothering to hide his amusement. I was happy to be entertaining him so much.

"I know that," I said, hoping that the withering tone would be enough to disguise the fact that I did in fact *not* know that before he spoke. "What I want to know is what is it doing in the ground?"

"That's the *kalua* pig," Hiapo said like he was explaining something to a child. Then again, in an altered state, maybe I was, because instead of really listening to Hiapo explain to me how the pig was cooked in a stone *kalua* oven in the ground, I was staring into the unseeing eyes of the pig, wondering to myself if they left its genitals intact.

The night became hazier from that point on, as if the extra alcohol I'd had from Hiapo suddenly caught up with me. The pork got passed around, and I remembered asking Hiapo if I could take the pig's head home and trying to get the hula dancers to show me the steps.

I have no idea what time it was when Maka helped me into his car, all I know is that I begged him to play "Barbie Girl" by Aqua on the way home. He complied, much to my surprise, and even played Ken to my Barbie in a really bad version of carpool karaoke.

I fell asleep in the car at some point and came to when Maka gently shook my shoulders. "Wake up, cutie," he murmured, his words not doing much more than passing through my mind. "We're back."

I fumbled with the seat belt for several seconds, confused as to why the latch just wouldn't release before I realized I was no longer buckled; Maka must have done it before waking me.

I managed to get out of the car by myself, even though the world felt lopsided. I closed my eyes, willing everything to straighten back up, to just go back to normal, but when I opened them again, nothing had changed. If anything, the ground beneath my feet felt even more crooked.

"Thank you for being a fun night, Maka, brah," I said, patting his muscled bicep.

Feeling worn out from the night's excitement, I stumbled off toward my apartment with its stupid lock that didn't know how to do its damn job. Someone needed to give the stupid thing a good talking to. Since it was my place, I guess that someone would have to be me. I was up to the task.

"Whoa, where are you going, exactly?" Maka jogged up to me.

"To my sleep so I can bed," I said, resisting Maka's grip on my arm. What did he have against sleeping that he had to keep getting in the way? First, he woke me up in his car, and now he was trying to physically come between me and my bed. What was up with that?

"Your new lock won't be installed until tomorrow. Back to my couch for the night."

I tried to keep my feet planted, but Maka was too strong, so I gave up and stumbled along with him into his apartment. Just inside the door, I nearly tripped over my own feet, and once again, Maka caught me, supporting me against his body, and once more, I noticed the body heat that roiled off him. Jesus, did he have a mini sun hidden beneath his skin?

"You know, you're really hot. Not physically—I mean literally hot. Temperature-wise."

"You don't think I'm hot physically?" Maka's beautiful lips—really, they were quite kissable, I decided—made an O of shock. "You might be the only one. That hula girl tonight sure did."

"That's not what I—I hate her," I added with venom. "Winky wiggling hula lady. Who goes through a crowd, winking at men just to get more tips shoved in her *up'a*—"

Maka nearly doubled over with laughter, and I stumbled out of his reach, sitting down shakily on the couch. "It's *pa'u*."

"Whatever, it doesn't—I'm getting off track." I shook my head, hands cupping my temples, trying to recapture my train of thought from the stingy hands of drunkenness. The alcohol struggled valiantly, but I managed to work at least some of it free. "I'm just saying that your body is warm. You have a lot of body heat."

"I've been told that before," Maka conceded, sitting down next to me on the couch, our knees and shoulders almost touching. "Some lovers didn't like it very much."

"I like it," I said quickly—far too quickly, the slowly sobering part of my mind said. It sounded like I was volunteering myself to be his lover, and while I didn't think I would mind filling the role, I didn't want to sound so desperate about it. "When I was with Trevor...I don't know, he was just cold. Not just emotionally distant, but his body was always cold. And the sex? Ugh." I let out a frustrated sigh and threw my head back, staring up at Maka's ceiling.

"Not good?" I didn't have to look at Maka to know that he was smirking. Hell, I'd have been smirking too, were I in his shoes.

"Not good at all. How do I say that in Hawaiian?"

"*Maika'i 'ole*," Maka supplied. "What was bad about it?"

I paused for a moment. It was a question no one had ever asked me before, so I didn't know how to answer it for a moment. I hadn't ever really tried to break it down in my own head, never searched for the trouble spots; I just knew it was bad. "Everything," I said at last. "He lacked passion. He was so...limp. It was just plain and boring and didn't even feel that good."

My brain became aware of Maka's closeness, aware of his smell, his own personal scent of cedar and male mixed with sweat and smoke from the *lū'au*. This god was sitting next to me, within easy reach, and I was sitting here thinking and talking about *Trevor*? What the hell was wrong with me?

"You, though," I said, trying to redeem myself and turn the conversation as far away from my incredibly awful ex as I could, "are the opposite. You're...hot, and just looking at you I can guess that you're passionate. You're probably amazing in bed."

It was the okolehao speaking and acting for me, I knew, but the alcohol was only acting on actual thoughts and desires in my mind. I couldn't deny my attraction to Maka, especially not with my subconscious rubbing it in my face with dreams like the one I'd had of him on the beach. A drunk tongue speaks a sober mind, right?

Maka peered at me through hooded eyes, a question in them that I didn't know, but knew I wanted to answer. "I've been told that."

Such simple words, but they sizzled over my skin like lightning bolts. Instinct drove me, and I closed the distance between us, pressing my mouth against his. I regretted it the moment our lips touched, but then he kissed me back—hard, searing, powerful—before breaking away, standing up.

Why? demanded the drunken voice in my head. *Why did we stop? He kissed back—why aren't we still kissing?*

"You need to get some sleep," he said, chest heaving, eyes wide as he looked at me. That question was still there in his eyes, but this time tinged with something else, something like regret. "I'll see you in the morning."

With that, he hurried into his bedroom and shut the door.

Chapter Ten

I KEPT MY eyes closed for several moments when I woke up, anticipating a rush of nausea or the splitting pains of a hangover headache. Surprisingly, neither came, and I opened my eyes tentatively, like a dog that doesn't quite trust the hand being held out to it.

Aside from not particularly enjoying the okolehao on my breath, I felt fine. I had that exhausted-from-not-sleeping-too-well feel, and my body ached from sleeping on the couch, but other than that, I was okay.

Physically, anyway.

Moments after opening my eyes, memories of the night before danced before my vision, each one seeming to taunt me with its stupidity. Did I actually refer to one of the performers as a winky wiggling hula lady? And how much had I actually begged Hiapo to let me take the pig head? What did Drunk Gabe think he was going to do with a pig's head? I remembered my miserable attempts at hula dancing and had vague recollections of getting upset when Maka had me return a large bundle of leis I'd spent the evening collecting.

They all paled in comparison, though, for without a doubt the most embarrassing memory from the night before was my conversation with Maka on that very couch, my pathetic come-on and then—sweet Jesus, did I really *kiss* him? I prayed that part was some alcohol-induced hallucination and not a true memory. It was too real, though, unfortunately.

"Gabe Maxfield, you are an idiot." It was an important enough statement that I needed to hear it said aloud to reinforce exactly how stupid I was.

I checked the time on my phone—which was on its last legs at two percent—and saw it was nearly seven. Where was Maka? Why hadn't he woken me up already, like he had the previous day? Did he leave the apartment in total mortification after my stupid kiss? Was he hiding from me in fear I'd kiss him again?

He kissed me back, a voice said quietly in my mind, though the rest of me pounced on it, squashing it silent because it was definitely not helping. It was right, though. I distinctly remembered him returning the kiss, for a second or two.

Maybe he was still sleeping? It was the weekend, after all, and surely even detectives got to sleep in.

I decided to figure it out later; at that moment, my bladder was screaming to be emptied after all the alcohol and pineapple juice I had the night before. I rolled to my feet off the couch, grateful the only aftereffects I felt were in my bladder, and tiptoed down the hall, just in case Maka *was* still sleeping.

I reached for the doorknob just as it opened outward, revealing Maka, a very thin, white terry cloth towel held precariously around his waist by his left hand. His body was still damp from the shower, a small cloud of literal steam flooding into the hall from the open door.

I was speechless. The way his hair fell, tousled and free of product, the way droplets of water slid slowly down his body toward the towel, the way the towel's thin material practically clung to his body, the way I could clearly see his cock outlined against it. All of it took my breath away.

"I didn't think you'd be up before noon, given the way you drank last night."

"I told you I can handle my alcohol. Ignore the fact that I wanted to carry the pig head home. Thanks for saying no, by the way." *Don't look down. Stop looking down. He can see you looking at his dick.*

"Did you really think I was going to let you bring a severed pig head in my car?" Maka stepped around me, making his way into his bedroom. As he walked through the door, he released the towel, exposing his bare ass, and I think I made a noise deep in my chest, but I couldn't be sure. If I did, I hoped to God he didn't hear it. My luck, though, he did.

I was hoping he would turn around, expose himself more, but instead, keeping his back to me, he pulled a pair of tight Andrew Christian underwear on over the round swell of his ass. As he lifted his leg to step into them, I did get a glimpse of heavy balls hanging low, and I thought I saw the head of his cock.

"It seemed like a good idea at the time," I said, mouth going dry for a reason that had nothing to do with drinking the night before.

Maka turned back around now to face me, and I was unable to resist looking down to see how his cock and balls looked hugged by the tight material. I doubted even someone with an iron will would have been able to resist looking at this work of art courtesy of Mother Nature and genetics.

"Red's a good color on you." Maka looked confused for a moment before looking down and seeing he was wearing red underwear. When he looked back up, I'm sure my face was as red as the fabric clinging to his body.

I'd never before been jealous of *fabric*, but I was now.

"Thanks," he said with a grin. "They better look good on me, considering how much they cost." Maka made a show of admiring his ass in them. If I had to guess, I would say that Maka was having a damn good time making me feel uncomfortable.

A sadist, I decided. *He's a sadist.*

"Well, uh." I cleared my throat. "I'm just going to—you know..." I pointed to the bathroom.

"The bathroom?" Maka filled in the blank. "That okolehao will go right through you."

I hurried into the bathroom and closed the door behind me, beyond embarrassed. It only got worse when I looked down and saw the blatant bulge in my pants where my stiff cock was pushing the fabric out. If I could see it then Maka could as well.

Kill me now. I would have climbed through the window in the bathroom, but it was far too small and my hips would have probably gotten stuck. I wanted to leave Maka's apartment with at least some of my dignity intact.

It's really hard to pee with an erection, but I managed, somehow. I emerged from the bathroom to find that Maka was in the small kitchen area, a pair of gym shorts pulled on over the red boxer briefs but still no shirt. Thank God for that small favor.

"I really feel like I need to apologize to you right now," I said, tapping the index finger of my right hand against my thigh, a nervous habit I had. That, and pacing; I couldn't keep my feet still when I was nervous.

"What for?" Maka asked, pouring water into his coffeemaker.

"For last night," I said, hoping he wasn't going to make me embarrass myself further by saying it out loud.

"Everybody gets drunk," Maka said dismissively.

"Not the getting drunk part. After." Maka turned expectant eyes on me, waiting. So he wasn't going to make it easy for me. *Definitely a sadist.* "I...when I kissed you. I clearly came on too strong, and you're not interested—"

"I don't have sex with drunk guys. At least not the first time, anyway."

"I hate the idea of throwing myself at a guy who isn't...the first time?"

"Are you drunk now?" The question was simple, but Maka's tone and the sudden, intense scrutiny he turned on me told me it was anything but.

I considered for a moment, feeling like it deserved a moment's thought. I'd certainly woken up drunk before, and this didn't quite feel the same. There was a strange headiness to the world at that moment, but I couldn't be certain that was because of the alcohol. "To be honest, I'm not sure. But I don't think so."

"That's good enough for me."

Maka closed the distance between us this time, one strong arm coming around behind my waist, pulling me flush against him, the other caressing the side of my face and tilting my head at the right angle for our lips to meet.

The contact sent fire rushing through my veins, hypersensitizing my body. The fingers toying with the hair just behind my ears sent tingles of pleasure through me, and the feel of our bodies, even through our clothes, had me moaning into the kiss.

I slid my hands up his bare chest, over his shoulders, and around his neck, trills of pleasure coursing through me. My fingers continued their path upwards, finally threading through Maka's hair.

When the kiss broke apart, we both stood there, clinging to each other and panting as we gazed into each other's eyes.

"That was probably a bad idea," Maka said.

"That's not what *this* says." I glanced down at the cock now straining against his underwear.

"You know what they say about thinking with your dick, right?"

"That it's way more fun than thinking with your head?" I grinned at him, leaning forward partly, inviting him in for another kiss—an invitation he accepted.

The hand he had holding the side of my face slid down, along my shoulder and then over my side to clutch at my ass, pushing my shirt up before slipping beneath the waistband of my pants.

Our tongues dueled, and we tasted deeply of each other, marveling in the sheer headiness of the action that was better than any alcohol. I needed to increase the physical contact, and my hands went down to his ass, cupping and squeezing the firm mounds of flesh.

Maka bit my bottom lip, the small jolt of pleasure-pain catching me off guard, and my cock throbbed hard in my pants.

"We should take this to the bedroom," Maka said, kissing my lips again between each word.

He would find no protest from me. I hurried along in front of him, tugging my shirt off as I went. Like Maka, I wondered if this was such a good idea, but any doubts I had flew out the window when I glanced back and saw Maka coming along behind me, his quite sizeable bulge leading the way. How could I say no to *that*? Could anyone who had eyes?

I reached the bed and turned around just in time for Maka to push me onto my back before mounting me on the bed. There was a hunger in his eyes, a primal one, and I was the full focus of it. The knowledge of that sent a shiver down my spine, one of anticipation and desire.

Our lips met again, but the kiss didn't last long before his lips moved down my jaw, to my neck, and then across my chest, alternating between kisses and sudden bites, and then his tongue swirled around my nipple. My back arched, and Maka chuckled.

"Like that?" he murmured against my skin.

"Uh huh," I answered, hoping he would keep going.

"Okay, what about this?" His tongue returned to my nipple, and then he bit down sharply, drawing a startled cry from my throat. I'd never had anyone do that before, and the crazy mix of sensations had me close to the edge already.

As he did it again, Maka's hand slid down my stomach to my cock, squeezing it firmly through my pants. "Get these off."

I complied, having several problems with my belt before managing to shuck them. Maka's hand took over when they reached my knees. "Someone is revved up," he observed, finger prodding at the wet spot slowly growing in my underwear. "Good. I like a guy who gets going."

I reached up, caressing his big pecs. I slid my fingers down to squeeze his nipples, which were almost as hard as his cock. He bit his bottom lip, closing his eyes with a sigh of pleasure. I pushed him onto his back and rolled my body half over him, repeating what he did to me, first on his right nipple and then on his left while he made encouraging noises. I kissed my way down, over his stomach, until I reached the waistband of his underwear.

I moved my lips along the side of his crotch, nudging his length with my nose, but otherwise paying it no attention. His scent swirled through my nostrils, infusing me, sending my arousal rocketing better and faster than any other substance could. It was like I was high on *him*.

I couldn't keep teasing him, and I finally mouthed him from root to tip, using my teeth to apply gentle pressure and tug at the fabric. I grabbed the waistband, and like he anticipated my next move, he raised his hips, allowing me to pull the underwear free.

"Jesus," I hissed when I saw him in all his glory. It was like the sex dream I had, the two of us on the beach. As I thought, his cock was long and perfectly shaped, just heavy enough to not point straight up, the mushroom head pushing out through the foreskin. "It's exactly like I dreamed."

Maka propped himself up on his elbows and looked at me, face cocky. "You had a sex dream about me?"

"Shut up," I muttered, dropping my eyes and taking his length in my hand, feeling its heat, its girth. *That* part was different from my dream, and so much better.

"I think it's hot," Maka went on, like he could sense my embarrassment. "Look at me. I think it's really hot. Almost as hot as seeing you down there with your hand around my cock, your mouth so close..."

"Close enough for this, right?" I licked the shaft gently, using just the tip of my tongue. "Or maybe this?" I trailed my tongue from just below the head down to his full, round balls.

"I like both options," he murmured.

"Then you'll really like this." I took him into my mouth then, savoring the length of it, the salty taste of it on my tongue—the way it stretched the muscles of my mouth. I took him as far in as I could, not stopping until his cock blocked the flow of air into my lungs and I had to fight back my gag reflex. It had been a while since I'd been with someone as big as Maka.

"*Akua!*" Maka threw his head back. I didn't know what the exclamation meant, but judging from his reaction, it wasn't a bad thing, so I redoubled my efforts, adding my hand, stroking the shaft as I worked my mouth up and down. Maka thrust his hips ever so slightly with my ministrations, so I threw my free arm across his hip, holding him in place.

He went along with me for a moment, letting me be in charge, but his personality wouldn't allow that to last. He rolled us once again, but didn't stop there; he took my shoulders and rolled me over onto my hands and knees, taking up position behind me. I lowered my head, peering at him upside down from between my legs as he removed my underwear.

Out of nowhere, he slapped my ass roughly, catching me off guard. I could feel the sting of it, and I hoped he would do it again. He attacked the other cheek, this time with his mouth, kissing, licking, and then biting it as he moved closer and closer to his target.

I closed my eyes, letting my head hang when his tongue finally made contact with my hole, wet and warm and wonderful. He licked in slow, lazy circles before finally diving full in, his tongue flicking rapidly against my opening.

It wasn't the first time I'd been rimmed, of course, but it had been a long time; pretty much the only thing Trevor liked to do sexually was hand jobs and penetration, and he wasn't that good at those. What Maka was doing in that moment, though, was a level beyond anything I'd experienced. He had my legs turned to jelly in seconds.

"Oh my god." I tossed my head back and forth. "Oh my fucking god!" I desperately wanted to reach down and touch myself, I was hovering on the edge from his tongue alone, and the slightest contact would push me over. I refused to be one of those guys who comes quickly.

"Feels good, huh?" Maka dragged his tongue lower, licking the back of my balls as his hand came down to grip my leaking shaft tightly.

"Amazing!"

Maka stretched his body past me, reaching to the nightstand. He removed a bottle of lube and a condom, and he placed them at his side before returning his tongue to my ass for a moment.

I closed my eyes in anticipation as I heard the lube bottle cap being popped open and the sound of the gel being squirted out. A moment later, the cold substance came in contact with my puckered hole, and I flinched against it before forcing myself to relax again.

Maka spread the gel around my hole with a fingertip. "You okay for this?"

I looked back at him over my shoulder, meeting his eyes and hoping he could see in them just how okay with this I was. "Please. I want you so bad, Maka."

He grinned, a wide, predatory expression. "That's what I like to hear."

He gave me no warning, just plunged his finger into me to the third knuckle. I cried out, arching my neck and throwing my head back in surprise. The penetration burned for a moment, an uncomfortable sensation that I was familiar enough with to know it would fade eventually.

After feeling my body relax, Maka began to move his finger in and out, removing it entirely before pushing it in once more. After I relaxed a bit, he added a second finger, scissoring them, twisting them around until the tip of his middle finger brushed against my prostate and sent waves of pleasure roiling through me.

"I can't wait any longer," I moaned, thrusting my ass back, grinding myself on his fingers.

"You think you're ready for this?" He slapped his heavy cock on my ass so there was no mistaking what he was talking about.

"Yes!" I shivered when he rubbed the head of his cock against my spit and lube-slicked hole.

Maka fumbled with the condom wrapper behind me, tossing it aside as he rolled the rubber down his thick length. As he applied lube to his cock, I focused on my breathing, deep and even. It had been a while, and Trevor had nothing on Maka in terms of length or girth.

My heart skipped a beat when I felt the blunt head pressing against my hole, testing the tightness. His hands slid up my back and then down and around, one stopping to tweak my nipple, the other continuing along my stomach until he gripped my cock, which had flagged a bit from nervousness. At his touch, it swelled to full erection once again, and Maka pushed in.

For a moment, the world went red, and I couldn't breathe. My ass burned way more than it had when his fingers were prepping me. I said nothing, though, gritting my teeth so he wouldn't stop or ask if I was okay. I'd much rather get it over with quickly and get to the part where it felt good.

I moaned when I felt his heavy balls push against my ass. He was completely inside me, and I had never felt so damn full.

"*Akua*, so fucking tight," Maka grunted, his hands sliding to grip my hips. He moved in and out slowly a few times, letting me adjust to his presence, but it didn't last long. He thrust harder, the sound of our bodies slapping together driving my arousal even higher. Every inward thrust pressed against my prostate, drawing moans from my lips. My fists knotted in the sheets, and my back arched to take him deeper.

I actually cursed when Maka withdrew from me, until he rolled me onto my back and pushed my legs up onto his shoulders. He looked down into my eyes as he guided himself against me, pushing inside with one smooth thrust, and I whimpered, reaching up and scratching my fingers down his chest.

Maka almost purred at the contact, moving his hips from side to side, thoroughly opening my body up and making me writhe beneath him, desperate for more contact. I grabbed his hips, trying to pull him deeper into me.

"Oh, you want something?" Maka teased, leaning down and nipping my neck gently. "What do you want, Gabe? Tell me what you want."

"More," I said through gritted teeth. "I want more."

"Oh? More what? More of this?" Maka pushed himself deep inside me, drawing a moan before he pulled almost completely out, leaving just the swollen mushroom head inside. "Is that what you want, Gabe?"

"Yes," I hissed impatiently, and Maka drove himself completely inside me once more. "Oh, fuck yes!"

"Say it," Maka demanded, once again nearly fully withdrawing from me. "Tell me what you want more of."

"Your cock," I moaned. My face was already flushed from our sex, so it couldn't get any redder, but if it could have, I would have blushed scarlet. "I need more. Please, Maka. *Please.*"

"Your wish is my command." He set a brutal pace then, his beautiful, muscular ass pounding his cock into me. He leaned down and captured my lips in a searing kiss, the full weight of his body on me, and I loved it. Every thrust had my cock sliding against his sweat-slicked abs, and I felt like I was damn near drowning in the sensation, and I desperately needed more.

I pushed on Maka's chest, and he followed my cue, rolling onto his back, hands holding my hips so I could stay on. The new angle had him pushing deeper inside me than before, and I started riding him hard, unable to quiet the moans, gasps, and groans of pleasure.

The look on Maka's face as I rode his cock was almost as sexual as the act itself, and I drew closer and closer to orgasm with every thrust.

"*U'i*," Maka breathed, moving me harder up and down on his length, his big hands squeezing my ass tightly before slapping it hard enough to blur the line between pleasure and pain, and almost unexpectedly, without touching myself, I came, erupting on Maka's stomach and chest.

Maka grunted as my muscles clenched on him, and he began drilling up in fast, brutal jabs, stopping when he was buried deep inside me and gritting his teeth before he finally went limp beneath me.

Legs cramping, I pulled off him and felt suddenly empty. Maka grabbed me, pulling me onto my side and holding me tightly against him, my head pillowed on his forearm. We both just lay there, breathing heavily and basking in the afterglow of sex.

"Next time," I said when blood was again properly circulating to my brain, "we do that in your hula outfit."

"Maybe we can make that happen," Maka laughed, caressing my arm and kissing my lips softly.

I rolled over, getting comfortable. As I lay there, feeling his chest rise and fall, I caught sight of another photo on his bedside table. I stretched out to grab it before I got comfortable again. The picture was of a girl in a beautiful dress, a bridesmaid dress, from the look of it. It was the same girl in the pictures out front—Maka's sister.

"Her name was Noelani. It means 'beautiful girl of heaven.' My parents doted on her. All of us loved her—it was impossible not to, honestly. You would have never met anyone as kind, sweet, or gentle. She was a perfect soul."

I smiled at the love in his voice as he described his sister, but stopped after I processed his words. "You said was."

Maka was silent for a moment, and I was afraid I'd gone too far. "She died nine years ago."

"I'm so sorry." I rolled back over to face him. His expression was wistful, bittersweet.

"Thanks. She had a rare heart defect. She was always weak, but it never stopped her from enjoying life, right up until the day she died. She was—and is, even now—my hero. She's actually the reason I joined the force."

Maka shifted his position, slipping his arm out from under me, no doubt because it was going numb.

I wanted to keep the conversation going, wanted to continue the connection that I felt at that moment, like a thread woven between us, tugging gently tighter and tighter the more we shared. "What do you mean?" I asked, placing my hand on his chest and massaging it gently.

"I never wanted to be a cop. I was a great surfer. My goal was to be a professional surfer, and I could have made it too." There was no bragging in his voice as he said it. He was simply stating a fact, and I had little trouble believing that he was great at it. I had trouble picturing him being bad at anything, actually.

"It was Noelani who dreamt of joining the police force. My parents couldn't figure out why; it seemed like a terrible idea for someone as kind and gentle as her."

Maka took the picture from me, smiling and caressing his sister's cheek. There was so much love in his gaze that I felt a stinging in my eyes and had to blink several times to keep them from tearing up. "When she died, I lost all passion for anything. For months, I could do nothing but dwell on her loss and how unfair it was. Finally I told myself that someone like Noelani, someone who loved life the way she did, she would be *pissed* at me for the way I was acting. How could I sit in the dark and hide from the world that she so desperately wanted to be a part of? So I got my shit together. The way I would honor her memory, I decided, was to do what she wanted to do. I joined the force and found I loved it, which surprised the hell out of me. I worked my ass off, climbing up the ranks, and here I am, top of the food chain as a homicide detective. That's my story."

I turned his head and gave him a gentle kiss. I didn't know how else to communicate the emotions I felt. I never did have a way with spoken words; I could express myself clearly and concisely if you gave me a pen and legal precedent to cite, but beyond that it felt like the art of communication utterly alluded me. Before anything more could be said, Maka's cell phone rang. He sat up immediately, letting my hand fall away.

"That's Benet's ringtone." He got up, naked, and padded into the living room. I heard his voice coming in as he had a conversation with his partner, though I could barely make out what was said.

He returned a little over two minutes later, his jaw set. He grabbed his underwear and pulled them up.

"I take it that wasn't a social call, then?"

"Call records from Carrie's phone came in. Turns out she'd had a pretty long conversation with someone a few days before her death." Maka pulled a pair of khakis out of a drawer, and though I was disappointed he was dressing, I was happy that I was getting to see the fabric of his underwear stretch over his ass the way it did when he bent down to retrieve them. "Before they actually talked, the same number called her twenty-four times this month, though it looks like she never answered. I'll give you one guess who the number is associated with."

He didn't have to say anything, and one guess would be plenty. After the finding that file, who could I think it was associated with other than this Delgado guy? I jumped out of bed.

"I'm going with you." This could be exactly what I needed to prove once and for all that Grace didn't have anything to do with this incident. I wasn't going to let the opportunity pass me by.

Maka looked me over, and I thought for a moment that he was going to say no, but instead he just sighed. "Well, you can't go naked."

Chapter Eleven

MANUEL DELGADO HAD an office located in the heart of the business district of Honolulu, a spire of glass and modern architecture. On the way there, Maka explained that Delgado was a businessman whose money came from property management, construction, and a few other odds and ends. Delgado was a respected member of Honolulu society, from all reports, and made a show of donating money to charity, as well as hosting fifty-thousand-dollar-a-plate charity events every year, and donating great amounts of money to the Democratic National Committee.

"I'm surprised there aren't billboards with his face plastered on them running for mayor or something," I muttered.

"There are no billboards in Hawai'i," Maka replied. "But yeah, if there were, then no doubt you'd see it. Most people think Delgado has political ambitions." Maka cut the engine and turned to look at me, eyes stern. "Listen to me, Gabe. You can come in with me, but you can't say anything. I mean it, you can't say *anything*. I'm not supposed to bring you here with me, technically speaking. I could get in a lot of trouble, so just stay quiet. Can you do that for me?"

"One silent treatment, coming up," I said, miming a zipper on my lips. "I'm serious," I assured him when he opened his mouth to speak again. "After this morning, the absolute last thing I want to do is get you in trouble."

Maka snorted. "That good, huh?"

Not caring that we were sitting in a parking lot outside of the office of a powerful businessman who quite likely sent someone to kill Carrie and attack me, I reached over and squeezed Maka's cock through his khakis.

Maka batted my hand away, but not before letting me get a good feel.

We exited the car, and I squinted against the bright morning sun reflecting off the glass tower. The interior of the building looked exactly how I expected it to: cold and modern, the floor reflective marble, everything designed to impress the greatness of this place—and by extension, the man who created it—on visitors.

A large crescent receptionist desk sat in the center of the room, and behind it an elevator and a staircase. It was Sunday, so there weren't many people going in and out of the place. There was, however, a secretary there.

Maka approached the counter, and I stayed few steps behind him so as not to draw too much attention to myself. "Excuse me, but I'd like to speak with Mr. Delgado."

The secretary glanced up at Maka, like she was weighing him to see how important he was before answering. She apparently didn't rate him very high, because her face remained impassive as she turned her attention back to her computer screen. "It's a Sunday."

"I already called his house, if that's what you're suggesting," Maka said, voice remaining polite. "They told me he'd gone into the office for a few hours and I could find him here."

"Maybe he just doesn't want to talk to you," the secretary said rudely.

"Looks pretty shady, him purposefully trying to avoid Honolulu PD," I commented and flinched when Maka shot me a glare. My statement worked, though, because the woman stiffened and turned to Maka with renewed interest.

"Can I see your badge?"

Maka complied, putting her at ease.

"You'll have to forgive me. Mr. Delgado gets a lot of people who come in with the next great project for him, or the next perfect charity for his investment, and they all demand to see him without an appointment. He's a very busy man, so it's my job to make sure that doesn't happen."

She picked up a phone and pushed two buttons. "Mr. Delgado has two visitors. I know. Honolulu Police." She was quiet for a moment, nodding at whatever was being said in her ear. "Understood. She hung up the phone and flashed her secretary's fake smile at us. "Mr. Delgado would be happy to see you in his office. Take the elevator to my left and go to floor eleven. His assistant will meet you there."

"*Mahalo*," Maka said, heading for the elevator. As soon as the doors closed, he stepped in close to me. "What did I tell you?"

"You told me not to talk to Delgado, not the receptionist," I pointed out. "Besides, I got us inside, didn't I?"

"You think my next step wasn't going to be flashing my badge?"

"Well, you were taking your sweet time," I grumbled, crossing my arms over my chest.

Maka turned my cheek so I was looking into his eyes, seeing how serious he was. "From now on, not one word. Not one, Gabe, okay?"

I nodded. "Okay. I promise."

The elevator doors slid smoothly and soundlessly open when we reached the eleventh floor, and, like the receptionist said, a man in a three-piece suit stood there waiting for us. No doubt he was Delgado's assistant.

"Good morning. I'm Tyson Ashburn, and I'm Mr. Delgado's assistant. I'm making myself available to answer any questions you might have. First things first, what is this in regards to?"

"That's between me and Mr. Delgado," Maka said firmly. "I was told I would be speaking directly to him. I appreciate your willingness to speak to us, but the only use I have for you right now is to have you lead me to your boss. That is, unless you want to be arrested for hindering a police investigation. And *that* certainly wouldn't look good for your boss, Mr. Ashburn."

Ashburn's face went beet red, like he couldn't believe Maka had the nerve to talk to him like that. I could barely suppress my smile, only succeeding by biting the inside of my cheeks rather forcefully. Unable to muster anything else to say, Ashburn spun on his heel, leading us down a hallway lined with a plush champagne-colored carpet until we reached two big double doors made out of a rich, dark wood with gleaming gold-colored handles in an ornate design.

It all reminded me quite a bit of my grandfather's office. When I was a child, I loved going there. Everything felt so big, so impressive, larger than life, just like my grandfather. There was a major difference, though. Delgado's office seemed to be entirely for show, another way of displaying just how wealthy he was. My grandfather, the splendor was for him. He didn't care about other people and almost never met anyone in his office. That sort of thing was reserved for a conference room that was not at all decadent.

Every step of this meeting with Delgado, from the dismissive attitude of the receptionist to the interference being run by the assistant, right down to the way the assistant grabbed the double doors by both handles and pushed them in at the same time, a gesture of grandeur—it was all designed to intimidate. I had no doubt that as soon as Maka called his house, someone phoned Delgado. The receptionist knew we were coming. This was all some game being played, and Delgado thought he had the upper hand. I prayed Maka didn't fall for it.

The office that Ashburn led us to would not have been out of place in a superhero movie featuring a billionaire villain. Everything reeked of money, including the large cherrywood desk behind which sat Manuel Delgado. He looked precisely how I pictured him: the body of someone who could have once been a manual laborer, who would have been at home in dirty, plaster-coated overalls or the cream-colored suit he currently wore. His jet-black hair was slicked back, a look that could have said *slumlord* but somehow said *dignified* on Delgado.

Delgado was on the phone as we entered or was at least pretending to be in order to delay us until he wanted to speak—another step in his game. He maintained his cool composure as he spoke on the phone, his eyes studying Maka and me with just the barest hint of interest.

Maka did not have a lot of patience for this man, and Delgado used it up quickly, judging by the way Maka stormed to his desk, took the phone from him, informed whoever was on the other end "He'll call you back," and hung up.

"That was a very important call with a client regarding groundbreaking at his work site," said Delgado coldly, lifting a bushy eyebrow in what probably passed as an intimidating look amongst his employees. His words were disdainful and his attitude dismissive, but there was some real steel beneath the surface, I noticed, an air of danger that I couldn't quite pinpoint, but made the hair on my neck stand on end.

"I told them you'd call them back," Maka said innocently. He wasn't going to intimidate easy. My already quite high approval of him soared even higher. A lot of people would have been quelled in the face of a man like Delgado. I was happy to see Maka wasn't one of them. "I'm detective Maka Kekoa with Honolulu PD, and I'd like to ask some questions."

"And your friend?" Delgado asked casually, motioning toward me. "You haven't introduced your companion to me. Would that be because he isn't a cop?"

I could not stop the flicker of surprise that crossed my face. It lasted only a second before I schooled my expression once more, but it was enough for Delgado, who chuckled and sat back in his leather office chair, fingers steepled together. He looked like he'd just won the first point in the match, and for some reason I agreed with him.

Maybe my coming here wasn't such a good idea.

"That really isn't relevant, Mr. Delgado. I'd like to ask you some questions in regard to the death of Carrie Lange. Perhaps you knew her?"

Delgado looked to Ashburn, who shrugged, expression blank. "I'm sorry, but I don't think I know who that is. The name certainly doesn't sound familiar to me. Was she a client of mine?"

"She was following you," Maka said. He dug into his pocket, pulling out his phone. "Do you recognize this number?" He held the phone out for Delgado to look at.

"I don't, no."

"What about you?" Maka held it out for Ashburn as well.

Ashburn grimaced, making him look constipated. "I believe that it is a number connected to this building, somewhere."

"Oh, somewhere? Let's be more specific, Mr. Ashburn. Where in the building?"

Ashburn flushed. "I wouldn't know off the top of my head."

"I would, Mr. Ashburn. From what HPD was able to determine, it's connected to the executive suites, so the number of people with access to those phones would be limited, right?"

I enjoyed seeing Maka at work; the assistant who had been so aloof earlier was now flustered and struggling to find words. A point scored for Maka, then. I expected Delgado to seem that way as well, but he looked perfectly composed, like evidence hadn't just been linked to him.

"I truly fail to see the point of all of this, Detective Kekoa," said Delgado, sounding bored.

"Let me fill you in, then." Maka stalked up to Delgado's desk, resting both hands on it so he could lean his considerably intimidating frame out, looming over Delgado. "A number connected to *your* office was found in the phone records of a woman who was paid to follow you and who has ended up dead. Why was Carrie Lange following you?"

"As I already told you, Detective, I don't know this woman, and if she were hired to follow me, I certainly wouldn't know why." Delgado straightened, the relaxed façade he'd been hiding behind dropping to reveal the steel I'd sensed earlier. "Do you have proof that I was being followed by this woman, Detective? If so, please get to it so we can stop wasting each other's time."

Don't say anything, Maka, I thought silently. If I was right and Delgado was connected, then he would know how I got the files and Maka mentioning them would create a lot of hassle for the investigation, not to mention potentially put *me* in more danger than I was already in.

"Can you explain why you called her twenty-five times this month?" Maka asked, effectively evading the other question.

"And where's your proof *I* called her?" Delgado spread his hands as if waiting for something to be handed to him or magically appear. "That number is not my office extension, Detective. I am hardly the only person who has access to the phones in this building. It seems to me that there is precious little evidence to connect me to the victim in either of the ways you are claiming."

Delgado's dismissive attitude and mannerisms—like he thought he'd already won the game—didn't put Maka off one bit. "Well, then, Mr. Delgado, why would someone from your office be calling a dead woman a few days before her death—a woman you say you don't know?"

"I hardly keep track of the personal lives of my employees, Detective, nor can I be held responsible for them." Delgado's voice darkened, something flashing behind his eyes. "I am a businessman who built my company from the ground up. I have worked tirelessly to make a name for myself and for my family, and I will not allow you to jeopardize that with wild allegations that have no basis in fact."

A knock came at the doors behind us, and I turned to see a man in a suit that looked like it cost more than my car and a year's rent at my condo combined walk in. He had salt-and-pepper hair and wore wire-rimmed glasses, the frame reflecting the light in what would have been an almost dapper manner if it weren't for the ugly expression on his face, like he'd just stepped in dog shit. Something told me Maka and I were the dog shit.

"I'm going to need you to address any further questions you have to me, Detective." The man's voice was higher than I expected, almost nasal, and very annoying. "I am Phillip Corbin of Corbin, Walters and Stein."

Maka shook his head at Delgado, a small smile on his face. "You weren't on the phone with a client. You were on the phone with your lawyer."

"Mr. Delgado is well within his rights to retain counsel when being questioned by the police," Corbin said haughtily. "I'm sorry that my client's knowledge of his rights inconveniences you. Now, I would like you to show me any evidence you have in regards to my client or this case."

Maka gave a short bark of laughter. "Are you kidding? No."

"Detective, if you don't hand over the information, I will be forced to file slander charges against you."

"No, you won't," I said before I could stop myself. I didn't look at Maka, not wanting to see his glare. "Slander charges can only be brought if the detective has spoken to someone *other* than your client in regards to this case, and a routine police investigation in pursuit of the facts doesn't fall under the category of slander. You can't prove damages, so there's little point. Besides, bringing that sort of charge would force a judge to review the information we have, which might lead to some uncomfortable questions for Mr. Delgado, and it would all become a matter of public record when we say what we believe your client's involvement is."

"Which would then become slander by definition, as other people would hear it," Corbin said fiercely.

"But court testimony is protected and can't be used to bring a charge of slander," I reminded the big-shot corporate attorney.

"Wrongful prosecution, then," Corbin snapped.

"I guess you could bring that up," I agreed sagely. "Of course, then I would turn to my friends at Hampton, Wyler, Morgan and Rodriguez for help. They owe me a favor or two." I dropped the names casually, knowing that a corporate attorney worth his pay would know exactly who my former bosses were. They'd made a name for themselves tearing down corrupt corporations and got very wealthy doing it.

I was happy to see Corbin's face pale, and he didn't say anything else, just watched me with a baleful look in his eyes. Well, if I accomplished nothing else today, at least I'd shut that asshole lawyer up.

"I think we've wasted enough of your time," Maka said, giving a polite nod to Delgado. "Have a lovely Sunday."

I kept waiting for the explosion to come as we left the building and got into the car, but surprisingly it didn't. Instead, when Maka finally spoke, he said, "That was some fancy legal talk. You sure you were just a paralegal?"

"I couldn't do my job if I wasn't really familiar with the law. People don't give paralegals enough credit." I waited until we were driving away from Delgado's office before speaking again. "What's next?"

"I'm dropping you back off at home. Your lock should get fixed today, so you can go home."

I frowned. "Is that your way of kicking me out of your bed?"

Maka could have given himself whiplash with how quickly his head turned toward me. "Are you crazy? No. I just meant—"

"Sorry," I muttered, embarrassed for overreacting. "It's just been a while, and I don't even know what you're looking for. Like, next-door booty call? Fuck buddies?"

"We're definitely not *fuck buddies*," Maka growled. "I know we need to have that talk, and it should be a long one, but I'll put this as plainly as I can, considering the time we have at the moment: I don't just want to fuck around. I'm too damn old for that."

"Good. Me too. I mean, that's also how I feel. How old *are* you?"

Maka chuckled. "How old do you think I am?"

"I feel like this is a trap..."

"I'm thirty-two."

"Oh, okay. Yeah, younger than I thought—ow!" I rubbed my arm where Maka playfully slapped me. Even being playful, his blows had some sting behind them. I reminded myself to be careful if I decided to wrestle him. "So you're taking me home, what then?"

Maka thought for a moment. "Actually, lunch first, and *then* I take you home. Then I meet up with Benet to see what progress he's made and if we can piece this damn case together."

"Okay, what's for lunch?" I asked, stomach letting out a little growl of anticipation. Until Maka mentioned food, I hadn't really been hungry; now, though, I was starving. "A burger sounds really good right about now."

"A burger?" Maka scoffed. "You're riding with a real Hawai'ian now, brah. I'm going to show you the best this island has to offer. I bet you've never had *laulau*, huh?"

"Laulau? What's that?"

Maka grinned. "You'll see."

"You know, you have this annoying habit of not answering questions. It's *annoying*."

"Why spoil the surprise?"

"Some people don't like surprises," I pointed out. "And I am one of them."

Maka patted my hand, each brief contact sending tendrils of excitement right to my cock. "Keep spending time with me. We'll get you used to it."

I very much liked the idea of getting used to it, but I wouldn't tell him that, at least not yet. That would come later. Maybe much later.

As he drove, it soon became apparent we were heading toward the beach, and my interest was piqued. "Let me guess," I said, to fill the silence, "this lulu has something to do with seafood?"

"It's laulau. And what makes you say that?"

"We're going to the beach."

Maka gave me an impressed nod. "You know, you actually do make a good detective. Yes, there is fish in it."

I tried not to show it, but I'm pretty sure I was glowing from the compliment.

It was just after eleven on a Sunday, so the beach was packed. Maka spent a solid five minutes looking for a parking space, but we finally found one. I was surprised when Maka cut the car off and got out. I looked around, but saw no sign of a restaurant.

"Okay, are we catching this *laulau* ourselves?" I asked as I got out of the car.

"*Laulau* isn't the name of a fish; it's a dish. I don't think we have the time to catch our meal ourselves. I could, though. Just throwing that out there."

I looked him over and grunted. "I just bet you could. If we're not catching it, where are we getting it?"

"Right over there." Maka pointed away from the beach, toward the back of the parking lot and a big yellow food truck I hadn't noticed before. "This guy makes the best *laulau* on any of the islands."

Once we were closer, I could read the truck: Big Eddie's Hawai'ian Plate Lunches. Whoever this Big Eddie guy was, his food was definitely popular. A line of at least fifteen people stretched from the truck, and it wasn't even officially lunchtime. "Judging by the size of the line, you're not the only one who thinks so."

"Don't worry, the line will move fast," Maka assured me. "Tell me, Gabe, are you a cat man or a dog man?"

The sudden personal question caught me off guard for a moment. "What?"

"Well, considering this morning..." He waggled his eyebrows to make sure I knew what part of the morning he was referencing. "I figured it would be good to learn a few things about each other. Myself, I'm a dog man."

"Me too. I had a Great Dane when I was a kid. Named him Marmaduke—real original, I know, but I loved him. He was the best thing about my family." I regretted the words as soon as they left my mouth, so naturally Maka zeroed in on them.

"You don't get along with your family?"

I shrugged, trying to keep my voice as nonchalant as I could. "I got along with my grandfather when he was alive, but other than that, no. My father is an entitled ass who never did anything for himself his entire life. He basically lived off my grandfather's name and expected that to carry him. My mother is possibly the least maternal person to ever bear children. I don't know what I was to her, but my theory is just a way to secure my grandfather's continued affection. My parents gave him a grandson, and he rewarded them by not writing them off completely."

"That's a little harsh, isn't it?" Maka reached the window, turning his attention to the scrawny Hawaiian man inside of it. He had a push-broom mustache and watery eyes and had to be close to my father's age. He had a big, booming voice, though, despite his apparent frailty.

"Maka Kekoa! Howzit? Been too long since I seen you, brah!"

"Big Eddie! You lookin' good as always, cuz! Howzit? Business boomin', yeah?" The sudden change in Maka's demeanor and words surprised me. He could slip so easily between professional and colloquial. It made me wonder more about his upbringing. I saw his point in asking questions.

"Who's the *haole*, cuz?" Big Eddie asked, drawing my attention back to their conversation.

"Big Eddie, this is my friend Gabe. Gabe, this is Big Eddie."

"Aloha," I said. "You're 'Big Eddie,' huh?"

"I'm a fan of irony," he replied with a deep belly laugh. "What can I get you two?"

"Two *laulau*," Maka ordered.

"Comin' right up!"

"When was the last time you saw your family?" Maka asked, as if our conversation had never paused.

"The day I left for college. Never went back home, not once."

Maka let out a low whistle. "Damn, man. What did they do to make you hate them so much?"

"Oh, you mean aside from a neglectful childhood where I was treated with the utmost indifference? When my grandfather died, I was sixteen. Knowing how my parents were, my grandfather set up my inheritance so they had no way of touching it—no legal access whatsoever. After he died, they tried to trick me into letting them have my money. When I wouldn't do it, they spent the next two years of my life making me feel guilty, making it known that if I didn't give them the money I was a terrible son and they wanted nothing to do with me. So as soon as I was able, I gave them their wish. They never need to have anything to do with me now."

"That's rough." Maka gave me a sympathetic shoulder squeeze just as Big Eddie leaned out of the window of the truck, carrying two Styrofoam food containers.

"Two *laulau*, like you asked," he said in his normal big voice. Then, in a lower, more conversational voice, he added, "Friend, huh? Not just any kind, though, right?" He winked at Maka. "You always did like those *haole*, boy."

"*Mahalo*," Maka said, holding up his Styrofoam container in thanks before strolling away back toward the car.

"Where are you going?" I asked. "You didn't pay!"

"It's all good. Now let's eat before it gets cold."

I jogged to catch up with him, cursing his long strides. "So, you like us *haole* guys, huh?"

"Yup," he said without missing a beat. "I guess I just like seeing those pale white asses spread wide around my dark cock."

Just like that, I was throbbing hard. "Yeah," I said faintly, "I bet that looks hot."

"Oh yeah. Why don't I make a video next time, and you can see for yourself?" He laughed at my look, hand very casually and discreetly brushing the front of my shorts. "Someone likes that idea, I see."

When we reached the car, we didn't get in, instead moving around to sit on the hood. "I present to you, *laulau*," he said triumphantly, opening his container, and I did the same. At first, it was hard for me to make sense of what I was seeing. Its smell was amazing, and it looked like pure goodness. I could see a tender strip of meat resting atop chunks of fish of some sort mixed with something resembling spinach, all nested inside a big leaf.

"Beef, butterfish, and taro leaves," Maka explained. "That's a ti leaf it's wrapped in. Eat it like a sandwich." He demonstrated by picking his up and eating about half of it in one bite. Shrugging, I picked up my own and took a bite, groaning in culinary heaven as soon as the wonderful taste hit my tongue. It was tender and salty and absolutely perfect, the meat and cooked taro leaves providing the best contrast of tastes and textures.

"Good, right?" Maka spoke through his second—and final—mouthful.

I grunted and nodded my agreement, not wanting to take any time away from chewing. Considering how amazing the food was, Hawaiian people must not make much time for conversation during dinner.

As I ate, I stared out at the beautiful Pacific, its glistening waves crashing against the sandy beach before pulling back. "God, the beach is beautiful," I said, using one of the cheap napkins to wipe my mouth.

"Correct me if I'm wrong, but there are beaches in Seattle, right?"

"There are, but they're different. Colder, kind of bleak. Good for a moody atmosphere. Not so great for seeing hunky guys out on the beach."

Maka faked a scowl. "You looking to eye some hunky guys on the beach, huh?"

"Not any guy in particular, no," I said, nudging him with my shoulder. "But it's nice to know that I have the option to do so, should the fancy strike me."

"How about I give you something different to eye when the fancy strikes you?" Maka suggested, his hand resting teasingly on my thigh.

"That might work." I slid my hand over the back of his.

Maka took my hand and pulled it over to his own lap, turning it so my palm was downward. My breath hitched when he dragged my hand right over his rapidly stiffening cock. I glanced around to see if anyone was looking, but the few people in the parking lot were in their own little world.

"I know a great place on the beach at night," Maka said, voice casual, like we were still discussing something trivial, like he wasn't slowly grinding himself up against my hand, his cock now completely stiff. I knew if I pulled my hand away, his cock would be perfectly outlined by the tight material of his pants. "It isn't a place tourists go, and most locals don't go there at night. Far away from the lights of the city, there's no concern about anyone seeing *anything*."

At the word anything, Maka placed his own hands over my now aching cock, a devilish half smile on his face.

"Anything, huh?" I asked, knowing I sounded breathy. I just couldn't force my lungs to act normal in this situation, couldn't be nonchalant with his strong fingers slowly and carefully kneading the length of my shaft through my shorts. It didn't help that his words reminded me of the dream I'd had of him. The opportunity to make that a reality...

Maka's phone rang, then, interrupting us. "Fuck. I need to take this. Give me a minute."

I watched him stride a few car lengths away, discreetly adjusting himself so his erection wasn't quite so obvious. I took great pleasure watching his body move, the way his muscles coiled and uncoiled with each motion. I wouldn't have described it as catlike; though he bore a certain grace, it wasn't feline. I didn't know what it was, but it wasn't that.

"Sorry about that," Maka said, rejoining me. "You finished with lunch? I hate to cut it short, but work awaits."

"All finished," I said, showing him my now empty lunch container. "And definitely worth the drive. I'll have to start being a frequent visitor of Big Eddie's."

We disposed of our containers in the garbage can set up back by Big Eddie's food truck and then returned to the car. Maka rolled down the windows and turned up the volume of the music as we reached the highway, singing loudly to a female singer who I didn't know.

"What?" he said, seeing my quizzical look. "You don't know Ariana Grande? Where the hell have you been?" He sang even louder, swaying left and right in his seat, even throwing in little finger snaps.

"You are so weird," I laughed.

"You know you like it. You want some of this, don't you?" He danced to the music in his seat, looking absolutely ridiculous.

I just shook my head, trying my best to smother the laughter. *Just when I think I'm starting to figure him out, something else comes up.*

"Since we're asking questions, I have one," I said. "The first day we met—when you helped me with the movers—after you left, the one you called Pako told me to be careful of you. Said you...god, what was it? You stay with the mad temper." Maka burst out laughing at that. "What? What the hell does it mean?"

"Just what it sounds like. Means I have a bad temper."

I tried to picture Maka with a bad temper. "I don't see it. What did you do to Pako to give him that impression?"

"Broke his nose arresting him," Maka said bluntly. "He tried to fight back, so I subdued him, and his nose got in the way. *After* he socked me in the jaw," he added quickly. "It didn't just come from nowhere, but I can see how he'd get that impression."

I blinked. "Wait, you're telling me the people who delivered my boxes were criminals?"

Maka snorted. "Just Pako. And nothing like theft or anything like that. Your things are safe, unless you had some weed in your boxes—in which case, it would be better not to tell me."

I wanted to make some kind of cute, flippant comment, but my phone vibrated loudly in my pocket before I could get the words together, making me jump. I nearly dropped the damn thing when I saw Grace on the caller ID. I couldn't believe my eyes. I glanced at Maka, who had a small smile on his face, and realized he knew. That would explain the phone call five minutes ago.

"Hello?" I answered, still not looking away from Maka's face. Yet another one of his surprises. I wondered what it would take to hammer home the point that I didn't like surprises. "Grace, is that you?"

"Who the hell else would it be?" Grace quipped. I saw jail did nothing to dull the edge of her acerbic tongue. "They set me free. I have been exonerated and ruled out as a suspect thanks to the official time of death, and the client with all the dogs dumping in her yard was able to corroborate my whereabouts. I'm a free woman."

"I'll come get you," I said quickly, my happiness overcoming anything I was feeling toward Maka at that moment. "I'm almost back to my place. I've got a lot to tell you."

"No, no, don't. I don't want to wait around for you to get here. I've spent enough time here already. I'll catch a taxi. Do you still have that film roll?"

"Yes, why?"

"I know how to develop them. Bring the film and meet me at the address I'm going to send you in a text message. We can see what was so special Carrie had to die for it."

I wanted to tell Grace to slow down, that she was just getting out of jail, so she should take some time before jumping into this head first.

When I thought about it, though, I could understand. Carrie was her coworker, and she'd been falsely accused of killing her. If I were in her shoes, I'd want to find out who was behind it as quickly as I could, screw taking time.

"Okay, see you there." Shortly after the call ended, I got the text message.

"Not off to do anything dangerous, are you?" Maka asked, concern in his voice. "Not breaking into any more houses?"

"Nothing like that, unfortunately." Instinct kicked in and I reached over, taking Maka's hand. The touch surprised him for a moment and then he intertwined our fingers, his thumb caressing the back of my hand gently. "Grace is going to develop the film we found. Maybe that will help fill in any blanks you and Benet come up with."

"We can't use the photos," Maka reminded me. "Fruit of the poisoned tree."

"I know the law. You know where they came from, but Benet doesn't, and I can get them to him in a way that keeps any pesky questions from coming up. Like dropping them off anonymously in the mail to be delivered to the police station."

"Let's not get ahead of ourselves," Maka said, turning the car into the parking lot in front of our condos. "We don't even know that the photos will be useful. Develop them and then we'll figure out what to do about it from there."

I made to get out of the car, but Maka caught my wrist. I looked back to see what he needed and he captured my mouth in a kiss that made my legs go limp. His tongue teased gently at my own, but it wasn't sexual or erotic—instead, passionate and sweet. It was, without a doubt, the perfect kiss.

"Wow," I said when our lips parted, unable to form better words for a moment.

"Be careful, and call me with updates, okay?"

"Okay." Even though all I really wanted to do right then was keep kissing Maka, I reminded myself that Grace was counting on me.

MAKA LET ME into his apartment to collect my car keys and the film roll, and then I was on my way to meet Grace. Thanks to all the traveling

I had been doing the last several days, I was getting to know the city pretty well. I didn't get lost once finding the building Grace referred me to. It looked to be a hobby shop dedicated to photography, a sign indicating that they had a darkroom.

The inside of the shop was lined with shelves of cameras, lenses, albums, and special printer paper. I didn't see any sign of an employee behind the counter. When I looked around, I didn't see anyone, either, but I did see a sign indicating that the darkroom was downstairs. Nothing said I needed permission to use it, so I followed the area and made my way down a set of creepy stairs that ended at a door with a red light next to it, currently off.

I walked inside the darkroom and to find a small rectangular space devoid of windows. Directly opposite me was a long row of tables, and on either side of those tables was a metal shelf lined with chemicals and materials needed for photo development, things I could make neither hide nor hair of.

On the wall just outside the door was a light switch panel with two switches. The upper switch turned on a single dirty yellow bulb. Light on, I stepped into the room proper, the heavy door swinging shut behind me. The noise of it made me jump, and I felt silly. It was just a door.

I pulled out my phone, sending a text message to Grace asking if she was almost here. I placed the film roll down on the long table for her, occupying myself by looking at the bottles of chemicals and reading their labels.

The door behind me opened just as I received a text message. "Wow, didn't take you as long as I thought it would," I said, glancing at my phone as I turned around. What I saw made me pause, my heart climbing into my throat. The message on my screen from Grace, which I expected to say something along the lines of *I'm here*, bore a different message.

Ten minutes out.

I rushed toward the table, reaching for the film, when a body slammed into me from behind, shoving me down over the table as a hand encased in a familiar black leather glove grasped the film container, the other hand pressing hard down on my head, holding my face against the table. I could smell the traces of the chemicals used before, like someone spilt them on the table and wiped them away without cleaning thoroughly. It made my nostrils burn and my eyes water.

I struggled against the body holding me down, grabbing for the film myself, but the hand on my head gripped my hair tightly, pulling my head up before slamming it down on the table. I saw stars bloom before my eyes.

The man must have thought that was enough to put me out of commission because he loosened his grip on me. I used that to my advantage, shoving myself backward, knocking him off-balance. As he recovered himself, I grabbed for the film. When he wouldn't let it go, I had no choice but to bite him, hard, going for the wrist where his skin was exposed. He cried out in pain, releasing the film, and I dashed for the door.

Upstairs. I just have to make it upstairs and I'll be safe.

Halfway up the staircase, I heard the door behind me open again. I quickened my pace, reaching the top of the stairs. I felt safe, but a hand closed on my shoulder, spinning me around as his other hand backhanded me hard, my head reeling from the blow. Before I could recover, he had me around the neck, shoving me against the wall and squeezing tightly, cutting off any oxygen. I thrashed out with my legs, trying to kick his knees in, but because of the angle he held me at, I couldn't get any real power behind the kick.

The man lifted me up with his hand around my neck and slammed me hard against the wall, knocking whatever air I had left out of me before letting me fall to the ground, where I sat, struggling to breathe once more.

I looked up at the man, determined to remember whatever I could about him. I saw through the ski mask that he was a white man with blue eyes. At least six feet tall, wide shoulders; I'd guess two hundred pounds or so. He was definitely the same guy who broke into my apartment to steal the file.

Before I could process anything else about him, he drew a gun from behind his back and aimed it straight at me—a headshot. He didn't want to hurt me; he wanted to kill me. He cocked the hammer back, and I closed my eyes, knowing there wasn't a damn thing I could do to stop him. This wasn't how I imagined myself dying. I thought I would die of old age, quietly in my bed, having lived a long and peaceful life with a man I loved—a man who could have been Maka, maybe, given the chance.

With the gun pointed at my face, the only thing I could think about at that moment was that I regretted not getting the chance to spend more time with the detective, not getting more insight into his mind, what made him tick, what made him happy, what made him sad. There was so much that I wanted to know about him, and now never would.

The next sound I expected to hear was the sound of the gun going off, so I was surprised when I heard a bell ringing as the door opened.

"Gabe?"

I opened my eyes in time to see my attacker turn toward the door. That was Grace's voice! "Grace, get out of here!"

The assailant took off running then, just as Grace appeared around a shelf loaded with photo printer paper. "Gabe?"

She turned her head when the sound of the bell rang again, and I cursed aloud. The film—the last thing we had that might connect Delgado to all of this—was gone.

Chapter Twelve

GRACE INSISTED ON driving my car to the police station, and I didn't argue with her. I was far too shaken up from having a gun pointed in my face to even think about getting behind the wheel of a car.

Grace tried to speak to me a few times on the way, but it just sounded like white noise; I couldn't get my brain to process anything she said. The one thing I could focus on was a question that gnawed at my brain, not letting go: how did he know I was there?

Had I been tailed ever since my house was broken into? Did this guy see what happened between Maka and me? Would that put Maka in danger? I didn't know; it all depended on if Delgado was the kind of person who would risk going after a police officer. He was dangerous, yes, that much was clear, but I didn't know if he would be that reckless.

It may not even be Delgado.

The thought would not have crossed my mind the previous day, but now I wasn't sure. The same man who broke into my house and stole the files attacked me once again, this time taking the camera roll? How did he even know it existed? That part didn't make sense to me. And even if he knew it existed, how the hell did he know where I would be going to develop it? Only one person, that I was aware of, knew.

I glanced at Grace, struggling to believe that I suspected her. What else could I think, though? She was the one who told me where to go. She knew about the film; she knew where I would be. According to Maka, she argued with Carrie about money.

Could my best friend be capable of this?

She has an alibi, I reminded myself, looking away from her and staring out the window so she wouldn't see what was going through my head. *She has an alibi, so she couldn't have killed Carrie.*

The thought comforted me a bit, but it didn't set me entirely at ease. Just because she didn't kill Carrie didn't mean that she wasn't somehow involved. What was going on? How had my life fallen apart so quickly in just a few short days? It didn't make any sense. All I wanted at that moment was to go back to the point in my life where my biggest concern was wondering when I was going to finally get a job and stop living off my inheritance.

Maka sat at his desk when Carrie and I entered the station. His desk was near the center of the bullpen, but it faced the door, so he saw us quite plainly. The look of surprise on his face initially faded to one of concern, and he crossed the room in what seemed like just a few steps.

"What happened?" He eyed my neck critically, jaw clenching. "Wait, don't answer that." He led Grace and me into a room marked Interrogation Room 1.

"Are we being questioned?" I joked nervously, looking around at the sparse room. Television got one thing about police work right, at least. The room was unornamented, the only thing in there a table with two chairs on either side and a camera. No two-sided mirror that I could see; whoever monitored the interrogation probably watched the feed from the closed-circuit camera.

"What happened?" Maka demanded again, turning expectant eyes on Grace.

I filled him in on what happened, refusing to meet Maka's face when I mentioned the attack. He was definitely pissed—I saw the veins bulging in his arms as he clenched his fists tightly.

"How the hell did this guy find you?" Maka demanded.

"That's a good question." I glanced at Grace quickly, looking away before she caught it. "Maybe the attacker has been stalking me since Friday night. They might have even been at the luau with us."

"You two went to a luau together?" Grace repeated, looking between the two of us. "Sounds like there's a lot you need to fill me in on, Gabe."

"Later," Maka said sternly. "For now we need to figure out who this guy is. Do you know if the shop has security cameras?"

Grace nodded. "It sells some pretty expensive items, so the security cameras are all functioning, as far as I know."

"Okay. Did either of you see any employees while this was happening?"

"I noticed the shop was empty when I first went in," I told him. "If there was someone in there during the attack, they would have heard the commotion and come to see what happened. I don't think anyone was there."

"That's really strange," Grace said. "Victoria is always there on Sundays. I don't know where she would have been."

"You're friends with the owner?" Maka asked.

Grace nodded.

"Can you give me her contact information? We need to get ahold of the security footage as soon as possible."

"Yeah. It's in my phone..." She trailed off, patting down her pockets. "Which I left in my purse in your car, Gabe. I'll be right back."

When Grace was out of the room Maka stepped close, pulling me into his arms and tilting my chin up so he could examine my neck. "Are you really okay?"

"I'm fine now. Scared shitless when it happened, but fine now." I glanced nervously toward the door. "I need to run something by you, okay? Before Grace comes back."

Maka listened as I confided my fears regarding Grace. I couldn't read his face, though, to tell what he thought about it. Once I finished, he sighed. "That's pretty complicated. But like you said, it's possible you were being followed from the moment the...items...came into your possession. Do you really think your friend is capable of this?"

"You did," I pointed out.

"No, I just followed the evidence. I don't know her, so I can't make that sort of judgment call. You can."

"Kekoa, you in here?" The partially closed interrogation room door opened, and Benet popped his head into the room. He frowned when he saw me, the frown growing to a scowl when he saw the way Maka held my arms.

I took a self-conscious step away from Maka, not wanting to get him in trouble at work.

"What do you need, Benet? Got something new?"

"Yeah. Finally tracked down those suspicious financial transactions the victim mentioned in her text conversation with Ms. Park." Benet waved a sheet of paper. "Also came across an address with no other identifying information found in her office, taped to the underside of a drawer."

"Let's start with the money," Maka said, taking the paper from Benet and looking at it. I craned my neck, trying to read around him without drawing too much attention from Benet.

"I highlighted the important part. Looks like three deposits of seven thousand dollars each were made into the company account and then withdrawn in cash from ATMs over the course of a week, a thousand a day."

Maka let out a low whistle. "Looks like the largest deposits they've ever gotten other than that are for a thousand dollars—and most are much lower. Where did this money come from?"

"That's a good question," I muttered darkly. The money matter made me feel even more uneasy. That much money coming into the company account would require access to withdraw, someone with a company card. I assumed that Grace and Carrie both used a company card when they were making purchases for their cases, which meant there were probably two of them. Who else would have access?

Why did everything start pointing to Grace suddenly? Or had it always done so, and I just didn't see it, blinded by the fact that she was my friend?

"Can I see this for a moment?" I snatched the bank statements from Maka's hand and stormed out of the interrogation room and through the front door, ignoring Maka and Benet calling out behind me.

Grace was just about to walk through when I emerged, brandishing the paper. "Did you do this? Did you?"

Grace stopped, clearly taken aback by my attitude, but I didn't care. "Did I do what? What are you talking about?"

"This money—the money that you and Carrie fought about. Did you do this?"

Grace reeled back like I'd slapped her. "No! Of course not! She accused me of it, and we fought, yeah, but I wasn't the one who did it! Do you think that if I was I'd still have a job? Carrie would have had me arrested without a second thought!"

"Look at this," I cried, shoving the paper into her hands. "Look at this and tell me you didn't. You have a company card, right?"

"Of course! It's standard practice, but...I didn't... Look, Gabe, I couldn't have!" She pressed her finger against the paper, forcing my attention to one of the thousand dollar withdrawals. "See? This proves it wasn't me."

I scanned what she pointed at, but couldn't see what she found so helpful. "What are you talking about?"

"Look at the time, idiot. The date, too. This is the day you arrived in Hawaii. This was an hour after you arrived—when you and I were eating dinner! Did you see me stop off at any ATMs? Whoever did this, it wasn't me."

"What about the photography place? You're the only one who knew I'd be there, and I happen to get attacked right after showing up?"

"You said yourself you've probably been followed since Friday night, so that's what happened. As for the missing employer," she added, addressing this part to Maka and Benet behind me, "I talked to Victoria, the owner. She's out of town this week, so she had one of her employees working today, a girl named Lea Harmon. She should have been there when we got there."

"Lea Harmon, was it?" Benet jotted down what she said. "We'll check into that."

"Do you recognize this address?" Maka asked, extending the second piece of paper to Grace, who mouthed it as she read it to herself.

"No. Why?"

"It was found taped to the bottom of one of the drawers in Carrie's desk," Maka explained. "We were hoping it might mean something to you. Maybe in connection to a case?"

"Sorry, wish I could help, but if it was one of Carrie's cases, she kept it secret from me. Like the Delgado case." She handed the paper back to Maka.

"We'd better get checking in on these leads," Benet said, stuffing his small notebook into his back pocket. "You two stay out of trouble now, you hear?" He jabbed a meaty finger at me and Grace. "Let's go, Kekoa."

Maka leaned toward me, cupping the back of my head and drawing our foreheads together. "Actually be careful this time, and don't just say you will be, okay?"

"Don't blame the victim," I said playfully, though I grew serious pretty quickly, seeing his expression. "I promise I'll do my best to stay out of trouble."

Once Maka and Benet disappeared into the building, I turned back to Grace, feeling uncomfortable with what had to come next. "Grace, I'm—"

Grace raised a hand to silence me. "Don't. There's nothing to apologize for. I don't blame you, considering everything that's been going on lately. I mean, you've been attacked twice in a matter of days. That's enough to make anyone suspicious."

She pulled me into a hug, squeezing tightly. "All is forgiven. Now—" She leaned back so I could see her face and the smile slowly spreading across it one I was quite familiar with. It was her crazy idea smile. "—I know you just made a promise and everything, but what do you say you and I go check out that address?"

"I'm pretty sure that would annoy Maka," I said hesitantly.

"Who cares if your boyfriend gets annoyed? He and that grouchy partner of his could spend all day tracking down bank things, and what if the answer to everything is at that house?" Grace shrugged at my hesitation. "I guess I understand you not wanting to piss off your new boyfriend."

"He's not my boyfriend. At least I don't think he is. And they took the address with them."

"I have it right here." Grace tapped her index finger against her temple. "I memorized it when they asked me about it. So you in?"

I didn't have to give it much thought. I wanted answers, especially now that I'd been attacked twice, and I wasn't going to get them sitting around on my hands. Besides, now that my attacker had the file and the film, there wasn't really a reason for him to come after me again. Except maybe unfinished business. I suppressed that thought quickly.

Grace misinterpreted my silence for refusal and shook her head with a loud *tsk*ing noise. "Wow, whipped that fast? He must have an amazing cock."

"Shut up. Give me the keys. I'm driving."

THE ADDRESS TURNED out to be residential, belonging to a home in an upper-middle class neighborhood. Cars lined the street in front of it, and I wondered what the hell was going on. In front of the house, we found our answer: a sign reading *Estate Sale Today*.

Grace and I traded disappointed looks, but decided it would be worth it to at least look around and see if we could find anything.

"An estate sale might actually be a good thing," Grace commented to me in a low voice as we approached the open front door. "It'll give us a chance to look around without raising suspicions."

The foyer and living room of the home were milling with people when we stepped inside, everyone engrossed in the elements of another person's life. Estate sales always struck me as distasteful; I understood their purpose, but to me, the people who showed up to things like this were like vultures, carrion birds benefiting from the death of another person. I needed to put my personal feelings aside, though, and focus on finding anything that might connect the owner of the house with Carrie.

Since the living room was unlikely to hold any sort of documents like we wanted to find, Grace and I bypassed it, instead heading upstairs where we were much more likely to find something. I noticed right away that there was no one else upstairs, but that wasn't necessarily a bad thing. Less people to see what we were doing, after all.

The first door that we came to was the bathroom, which we ignored. The next room looked like the master bedroom, which seemed as good a place as any to start. No sooner had we stepped through the door, though, than a voice said, "The upstairs is off limits."

Grace and I cringed for a moment but schooled our faces into apologetic expressions and turned around. A young woman, no older than nineteen or twenty, stood in the doorway, arms crossed over her chest. Her eyes were puffy and red, her face still showed evidence of recent crying. She was at least partially Hawaiian, judging by her hair and eyes, though her skin was pale and white.

"I'm so sorry," I said quickly. "We didn't realize. We must not have been here when they made that announcement. I'm sorry for your loss," I added. "I know it can seem a little barbaric, all these people swarming over your belongings right after a loss."

"The lawyer said this was a good idea, but I couldn't bring myself to get rid of everything, so I only agreed to sell the things in the living room and kitchen. This is—was—my grandmother's room. She died a week ago from a heart attack."

"That's awful," said Grace sympathetically, digging into her purse and offering a tissue, as it looked like the woman was about to start crying again. "You were clearly close."

"After my father died a year ago, my grandmother was all that I had. Now I don't have anyone." I saw her swallow back the beginning of a sob, wiping her hands beneath her eyes quickly to prevent any tears from falling.

"I don't know how you can bear it, two losses so close together. You're very strong, Ms.—I'm sorry, I don't think I got your name?"

"I'm Lana. Lana Brighton."

"I'm Grace Park, and this is my friend Gabe Maxfield. I'd like to be honest with you, if that's all right? We work for a company called Paradise Investigations."

"The private detectives my grandma hired?"

"Well, we work with the private detective your grandmother hired," I said, hope flowering in my chest. "We were hoping you could discuss the case with us. You see, our partner recently passed away, and we're trying to consolidate as much information as we can about the cases she was working on."

"I don't know anything about it, really. Grandma couldn't get over my dad's death. He died in a car accident, but she was convinced that he was murdered by his boss or something."

My eyes widened at that, and I gave Grace a meaningful look. She nodded her understanding. Lana seemed oblivious to us and kept talking.

"I tried to convince her she was being silly, but she just wouldn't let it go. About a month ago, she told me she had hired a private detective to look into the case. Until the very end, she wouldn't let it go."

"Can you tell us your grandmother's name?"

"Miriam Brighton."

"You said she was convinced your father's boss murdered him, right? Where did your father work?"

Lana thought for a moment. "I think it was called DLC Construction."

"Do you—" Grace started, but I grabbed her hand, pulling her behind me out the door.

"Thank you very much for your time and candor. We'll see ourselves out."

Grace struggled against me the whole way down the stairs, finally pulling free once we were out of the door. "What was that all about?"

"I was there today," I said impatiently, speed walking to my car.

"Where?" Grace asked, hurrying to keep up.

"DLC Construction. That's Delgado's company."

"Where are we going now?" Grace demanded, bracing herself on the door of the car as I sped away from the curb in front of Miriam Brighton's house.

"To your office. We need to find the file on Miriam Brighton and see what it has."

"We don't know that there *is* a file," Grace argued. "It was probably the file that got stolen from you."

I shook my head. I didn't know why I was so certain, but I was. "That file was marked Delgado. Even if it was all of the information she collected, there has to be some record of Miriam Brighton, right? Especially if you got paid by her."

"You're right, but I wouldn't begin to know where to look."

"Well then, call Peter and have him meet us there."

Grace face-palmed lightly. "Why didn't I think of that?"

"Because I'm smarter and prettier than you are," I said, smirking.

As Grace talked to Peter, I debated whether or not to call Maka. He said he wanted updates, but he also told me to be careful, and I didn't know if he would consider continuing an investigation independent of the police being careful. Considering what had happened the last few times I'd done so, I didn't think he would approve. I decided it would be beg forgiveness than to ask permission. If we discovered anything, I could tell him. If we didn't, then I wouldn't need to.

About five minutes out from the office, Grace got a text message. "It's Peter. He's at the office waiting for us. He's started looking for the file."

"Good. Hopefully he finds it before we get there." I didn't say it out loud, but I didn't look forward to returning to that place. I didn't think anyone would be able to blame me, after discovering the body of a murdered woman. I'd already met Peter there once, and that was enough. I wish I'd known about Miriam Brighton then and could have been spared all of this extra trouble.

"We don't even know that there's going to be a file there," Grace said suddenly. It sounded like something she'd been mulling over for a while before speaking. "Someone tore her office up; they probably took the file that day."

"Not if they were only looking for things specifically marked Delgado. Whoever they were, they might not have known the name of the person who hired her. If that's the case, then there's hope the file is still in there."

"Well, we won't know until we get there." Grace drummed her fingers impatiently on the door.

When we pulled up in front of Paradise Investigations, Grace basically leapt out of the car before it had even stopped. I hadn't seen her this determined since her professor told her that she had no chance of passing the class. She'd proven him wrong. When she got like this, she could accomplish damn near anything. I didn't fully understand what her relationship with Carrie was like—but Grace was motivated to find her killer, and I felt sorry for anyone who tried to get in her way.

Inside the front office, Peter had dragged out several cardboard boxes and was going through one, discarding files one by one.

"Grab a box," he said, gesturing to the small pile of them.

"Hello to you, too," Grace muttered, squatting down over the nearest box. "It's not like I just got out of prison or anything."

"Jail," I corrected, sliding my own box toward me and tossing the lid aside.

"Do you really want to argue semantics with me on this right now?"

"No, no, you're right. Either place is terrible," I said placatingly before Grace could get worked up. None of us would be able to accomplish anything if she got started in on a rant.

I started digging through the box, reading the file names and discarding them quickly. With every file I put aside, my uneasiness grew. *Please be here*, I silently prayed. *Please be here.*

It was boring work, and my back soon ached from sitting on the floor with no support. I dragged my box to the sofa and sat with my back against it, which felt a little better. I just managed to get comfortable when my phone vibrated on the floor over where I had been sitting.

"Son of a bitch." I got up once more, retrieved the offending device, and sat back down.

The vibrating came from a message from Maka.

At the bank where the withdrawals were made. Accessing the ATM camera footage now. Hope to have an ID soon.

That's great! I typed back. *Me and Grace are with her secretary at their office looking through files for anything useful. I'll let you know if we find anything.*

"Found it!" Peter held a manila file folder up triumphantly. "Brighton, Miriam."

"Great job, Peter," Grace cried. "Let me see that." She took the folder and opened it. "Jesus, there's almost nothing in here. Looks like it's just the initial interview notes. Listen to this: 'Client believes that the death of her son, Laurence Brighton was not an accident as previously reported. She claims that her son was a former employee of DLC Construction, and that he'd recently quit. According to the client, he was in possession of evidence of illicit activities that would be damning to the company owner, Manuel Delgado. As to the nature of this evidence, she did not elaborate. It is her belief that Delgado or agents working on his orders staged the murder of her son to look like an accident in order to keep him from approaching the police with this information. She is requesting that evidence of this be found and taken to the police.'"

"That matches what the granddaughter told us," I said, glancing over Grace's shoulder at the paper. "Look at the date of the consultation: two months ago. She'd been working on this for a while."

"She must not have found anything, then," Peter said, climbing to his feet and dusting off his pants.

"What makes you say that?" I asked, cocking my head at him.

"If she had, it would have been taken to the police, right?"

"Someone murdered her over that file," Grace argued. "And almost murdered Gabe, too."

"Twice," I interjected.

"They wouldn't have done that if they didn't think she stumbled onto anything. They were intent on stealing that file."

"And now that they have the film, too, there's no hope of proving it, huh?"

Grace blinked in surprise. "You knew about the camera roll?"

"Yeah. Gabe has kept me filled in on what he's found, since you sent him my way to find out more about Carrie's death."

"That was smart thinking on his part," Grace said, though her voice sounded strange. I didn't ponder it too much, though, because my phone rang.

"Sorry, guys. Just a sec." I turned my back on them, answering Maka's call. "Hey, Maka. Get an ID?"

"We did," Maka said, voice thick with urgency. "Gabe, where are you?"

"I told you, we're—"

"If you're still with Peter, get out of there! He's the one who withdrew the money. *It's Peter.*"

Chapter Thirteen

"HANG UP THE phone, Gabe," Peter said behind me, his voice frigid. I turned around slowly, stopping in my tracks when I saw that in his hand he had a gun. "I said hang up the damn phone!"

I clicked end, holding out the phone to show him that I'd done as he asked. This was the second time today that I'd had a gun pointed at me, and I had to say I didn't like it now any more than I had the first time.

There was something different about the situations, though. The first time the man holding the gun looked more than willing to pull the trigger. Calm, collected, a man who'd definitely killed before. Peter, on the other hand, looked nervous, frantic, like the world around him was falling apart. He was stressing out in a situation that had gotten beyond him.

"What's going on, Peter?" Grace asked, stepping back so she was standing beside me.

"Shut up!" Peter shouted, and we both flinched. "Turn your phones off and toss them on the floor!"

Grace looked like she was about to give him sass, so I elbowed her hard, doing as he asked with my cell phone and glaring at her until she did, as well. I was not about to get shot because of Grace's fiery temper.

"Did you kill Carrie?" Grace asked after she'd tossed her own phone aside. "Peter, look at me. Did you kill Carrie?"

"It wasn't supposed to happen like that!" he shouted, pacing the floor in front of us. I kept my eyes on his gun as he walked, waiting for him to lower his guard so I could take it. "She didn't have to die! She wasn't supposed to be here!"

"You were the person withdrawing the money," I said, keeping my words neutral, my tone soothing. I made it an observation, not an accusation.

"I was approached by a man who said he'd pay me money for information. First he just wanted to know who was trailing his boss. He paid me seven thousand dollars to find out. I knew it would be flagged by the bank if I had it put into my account. A business account, though, it wouldn't be noticed. I had a third business card issued in my name, and withdrew the ATM limit of one thousand dollars a day."

"The second time?"

"He said he'd pay me fourteen thousand dollars to bring him whatever files Carrie had on his boss, Delgado. Before all the money could clear, though, Carrie started getting suspicious, so the last seven thousand I transferred to a friend's account, giving them a thousand dollar cut. When the money cleared, I started looking for the file. For some reason, Carrie came back to the office. She...she found me searching. She was furious. We got into a fight, and I...I killed her."

"She came back because of the money," I told him. "She had an alert set up so she could catch Grace stealing the money. When the money transfer happened, she got a text message and rushed back here. If you hadn't transferred the money that way, she might not have ever come back here."

"Why did you do it, Peter?" Grace asked. She didn't sound angry; she sounded sad, disappointed.

"Why?" Peter shouted, rounding on Grace, leveling the gun at her. "*Why*? Do you know what it's like to be drowning in debt? With what I made here, I couldn't even start to get out of the hole. If I'd paid every bill I'd have used my whole paycheck and still not have been caught up every month!"

"If you were having money problems, why didn't you say anything?"

Peter laughed bitterly. "I did! I asked Carrie for more money, just a couple hundred more a month, that's all I needed. You know what she told me? 'You're well compensated here, and we can't afford to pay you any more than we already do.' Can you believe that?"

"Well then, why didn't you come to me? I could have—"

"You could have what? Loaned me thirty dollars? Everyone knows you're not the one with money, Grace, so don't kid yourself. I did what I had to do. Everything would have been fine if Carrie hadn't come back when she wasn't supposed to!"

"Would it?" I asked, trying to keep him talking, praying that Maka and Benet were on their way. "The file wasn't here, so you wouldn't have been able to give it to them, even if Carrie hadn't come back. What would have happened then, Peter? Do you think a man like Delgado, a man willing to kill for information, would have just let that slide? Use your head. Everything hit the fan, and you're a loose end now. Even if you get away with all this, Delgado is probably going to have you killed so you can't come back to haunt him later."

"Shut up! Shut up, shut up, shut up, *shut up!*" Peter screamed, nearly in hysterics. He was fast approaching a breakdown, and I didn't know if that would be good or bad. I had to try *something*, though.

"Why didn't you go to Carrie's house and look for the files after you didn't find them in the office?" I asked, all the while telling myself, *Just keep him talking. Just keep him talking.* "Wouldn't that have been easier? Why get the hired help involved?"

Peter scowled. "That wasn't my idea. The house, though, it made sense, right? The police arrested Grace, thinking she did it. If I ransacked Carrie's house, they would know Grace wasn't guilty, and that would have just fucked up the plan. If the police got the files, it would have fucked everything up, too, but that was for the guy with the money to figure out. And then, somehow, Gabe got to the house just hours before the police did and managed to get his hands on the files. I was happy, the boss was happy, and the plan kept working."

"The plan," Grace derided. "What's the next step in the plan, Peter? Where do you go from here now that Gabe and I both know?"

"The plan? The plan now is to kill your little friend here and pin it on you. My story will go something like this: I showed up right after you shot him, we wrestled for the gun, and then, to save my own life, I shot you dead. The police will believe me, you know. They already suspect you anyway."

Peter raised the gun, pointing it at my head. I felt like I was going to throw up. Part of me wanted, like earlier, to close my eyes, but I didn't want to give up or surrender to death, not at the hands of *this* man.

"Tell me about the camera roll," I said quickly. "I still don't understand how you knew where I'd go to develop it."

Peter snorted. "If you wanted Grace's advice, that's where she'd tell you to go. I told Delgado's people they just needed to stake it out."

"But how did you know when we'd be there?" I pressed, straining my ears to catch the sound of police sirens. They were coming, right? They had to be. Maka knew where we were and knew Peter was here, so they would get there. They had to. "I didn't know until today, and yet the guy was ready for me, and the shop was empty."

Peter waved the hand holding the gun dismissively. "That was easy. I cloned Grace and Carrie's phones a long time ago—it's how I figured out which of them was working the Delgado case. I monitored the texts, and when she told you where to go, I got there first. The shop girl, whatever her name was, she was a cute girl, so it wasn't too hard to distract her for a little while. Convinced her to take me to the stockroom for a little fun."

Grace scowled. "So you're a rapist and a murderer?"

"What? Dear god, no. It was one hundred percent consensual. Despite what you may think of me, I'm not a monster."

"That's debatable," I said.

Peter turned on me, growling through gritted teeth. "What did you just say?"

I spoke much slower than necessary, knowing he would pick up the perceived slight. "I said that's debatable. You're a monster, no matter how you try to justify it to yourself."

"You stupid son of a bitch!" Peter hit me across the left side of my head with the gun. Luckily for me, it was a glancing blow; he obviously didn't have much experience with a gun. It still hurt like hell, though.

Grace took her chance, grabbing for the gun in Peter's hand. The two struggled, pulling it this way and that, and I feared it would go off at any moment. *Where the hell is Maka?* If the police didn't get there soon, the situation was going to spiral even further out of control than it already had, and someone was going to end up dead.

And then, just like that, somehow Grace had the upper hand. She jerked the gun out of Peter's grip, holding it aloft from him. Peter, though, was fighting with the strength of a desperate man. He grabbed Grace around the waist, lifting her up and slamming her down on his desk, face purple with his rage.

Grace lashed out, fingernails scoring two deep lines on Peter's cheek. He laughed wildly, picking up the small name plaque on his desk and slamming it across Grace's face. Disoriented, she released the gun, and Peter took it from her.

"Peter," I pleaded, watching him take a step back from her, right hand holding the gun at her chest, left hand coming up to dab at the blood seeping from the scratches on his face.

The wild laughter came again as he examined his fingers. "Thanks for legitimizing the struggle story I'm going to weave, Grace. You just made me that much more believable."

"The police know who you are!" I shouted when he cocked back the hammer.

Peter didn't even look at me. "You're lying."

"No, no I'm not. That phone call I got earlier was from one of the detectives who went to see you the day I first met you." I was talking fast, praying that he listened to me and that he would get spooked and maybe flee without harming either of us. "He and his partner went to the ATM where you withdrew all the money, and they got the footage. The call was him telling me you were the one withdrawing it. They know, Peter, so this whole crazy 'she killed him I killed her in self-defense' thing isn't going to work. They're on their way. They'll be here any minute."

Face blanching, Peter glanced over his shoulder at the window behind him like he expected to see the police cars pouring into the parking lot. It was the briefest moment of distraction, but it was my opportunity, and I took it. I lunged at him, hitting him around his knees, and he fell to the ground with a loud cry, the gun skittering across the floor.

I scrambled past him on my hands and knees, making for the gun, but he grabbed me by the ankle and jerked me back hard. My chest and chin hit the carpeted floor, jarring my teeth. I kicked my free leg out, making contact with some part of his body—I heard his *oof* of pain and managed to tug my other leg free of his grip. The gun was almost within my reach. If I could get it, I could bring an end to this nightmare, hold Peter at bay until the police came.

But what if he tried to run? If he got away, then it wouldn't be over. If he got away, Grace and I might still be in danger. I couldn't let that happen, but could I shoot him if it came to it? I'd never shot a gun before in my life, and I didn't think I could take a man's life. Granted, I'd never been put in a position before where it might be necessary.

"Gabe!" Grace cried just before I felt something thin and hard slam down on the middle of my back. Pain lanced through me, and I rolled over in time to see Peter raising a chair above his head to bring down on me again. I lifted my feet, catching the chair at the bottom and keeping it at bay before thrusting upward and sending the chair flying from his hands. I tried to roll over to get the gun, but Peter stomped on my stomach, making me double over.

He used that time to grab the gun and back away from me, pointing it at me, his eyes wide and crazed. "Get over here," he snapped at Grace. "Get the fuck over here!"

"Okay, okay, just stay calm," Grace said, holding her hands up in surrender. She climbed off the desk and made her way over to the wall next to me, sitting down.

I pushed myself into a sitting position next to Grace, glaring up at Peter. It was all over, I knew, but I would not go out a coward. I would not close my eyes to this man, as I had to my assailant at the photography shop. I would look Peter square in the face as he pulled the trigger.

"You couldn't just stop looking around, could you? Couldn't let it go? You got Grace off on her murder charges; why couldn't you be satisfied with it? It was over. It was *over*. But no, now you both have to die."

Peter pointed the gun at me once again, cocking the hammer back. He moved the gun between us, back and forth, like he couldn't decide which of us he would shoot first, or he was just playing some sort of psychological game with us. At that point, I wouldn't have put it past him.

"Just do it," Grace sneered. Had she gone insane? Was she taunting a murderer into actually shooting us? "Go on, just pull the trigger! You say you're going to shoot us, so just do it! Stop playing games!"

"You think I won't?" Peter cried, turning the gun on her. "You think I won't do it?"

A loud noise very different from what you hear on television left my ears ringing. Bits of wall and plaster sprayed out from a hole in the wall halfway between Grace and me.

He really is going to do it. My heart beat erratically in my chest as those words bounced around my mind again and again. They say your life flashes before your eyes, but that didn't happen for me. Maka did, and the short amount of time we spent together. I wished for more—more time to get to know him. More time to see his goofy side. More time to learn just where he liked to be touched, what made him feel the best. What foods he liked—or, probably a better question, what foods did he *not* like? It was unfair, having such a short amount of time with him.

For the second time, I heard gunshots, and my body spasmed, like it anticipated receiving the shot; why wouldn't it? I registered nothing for several long seconds—like time had stopped, everything frozen in one brief moment, like someone had pushed the pause button on existence.

My mind couldn't recall who the gun was pointed at—was it me, or was it Grace? Shouldn't I be feeling *something* right now? It hurt to get shot, right? Unless I was in shock—I could have been in shock, I guess. The fact that I was thinking meant I was still alive, right?

And then someone pressed play and reality kicked back in. Blood blossomed on Peter's shirt, spreading out in a slow, dark patch. The gun fell from his hand, clattering heavily to the floor. Peter's face was a mask of surprise. He looked down at his chest, touching at the blood. I could practically see his mind trying to make sense of everything.

He fell slowly to his knees. Peter opened his mouth to say something, but only a gurgle of blood bubbled out. I looked over his shoulder, not believing this was actually happening, and saw Maka standing there, his gun drawn and pointed where Peter had been standing.

I was alive. A quick look at Grace told me she was fine too. We were fine. We were fine, and it was over.

Chapter Fourteen

FIFTEEN MINUTES LATER, I sat in the backseat of Maka's car, the door open. I couldn't get my arms and legs to stop shaking—shock, the medic said. Benet stood over me, asking me questions while Maka did the same to Grace.

"What happened next?" Benet asked in his usual gruff voice.

"Remember how I told you that you that you should work on your bedside manner?"

"Just answer the question."

"Then he told me to put the gun down, proceeded to confess to why he killed Carrie—"

"Which was?"

I sighed. I didn't want to relive it, but I knew that I had to at some point, and now was probably better than later. I walked him through everything that happened, repeating Peter's words with as much accuracy as I could. I stopped a few times to think through the order of events, before continuing, but eventually I got to Maka shooting Peter.

"You know the rest," I finished, exhausted just from the few minutes spent going over the story.

Maka, finished with his interview of Grace, came over to the car. Benet glowered at him in his surly way and lumbered off. Maka rested his forearm on the hood of the car, leaning down to look at me, his face etched with concern.

"I'm fine," I said before he could ask. "Just..."

"Scared?" Maka supplied.

"Tired," I corrected. "Though, I won't lie, I was scared in there."

"There aren't many people who wouldn't be, looking down the barrel of a gun, particularly when it's being held by a cornered man. I know I would be."

"Thank you," I said suddenly. "If it wasn't for you, I'd be dead right now. Grace and I both would. You saved our lives."

"I did my job," he said. "Nothing more and nothing less."

"Well, thanks to your job, I'm alive. I owe you."

Maka waggled his eyebrows. "You mean, like, a great blowjob?"

I mustered a small smile. "Well, I have been told I am an expert on those."

Maka smiled too.

I WOKE UP to warm, wet kisses trailing down my neck. When I opened my eyes, it was already dark outside, and I had no idea where I was. Disoriented, I thrashed a bit, only to be soothed quietly by Maka's gentle hands, his lips pressing into the space just behind my ear, his breath ghosting across my neck.

"It's okay. I'm sorry. I didn't mean to scare you."

Memories came back, and I sat up. After the incident at Paradise Investigations, Maka had a uniformed officer drive me back to his place in my car, tailed by his partner so he could leave afterward. I let myself in the apartment with his spare key and then passed out on his bed.

"You didn't lock the door," he chided me gently.

"Sorry. You're lucky I even made it to the bed before passing out." I stretched, rolling over and nestling against him, taking strength from his warmth. "How can I be this tired after sleeping so long?"

"You went through a lot today," Maka said, his warm palm making small circles against my back, lulling me back into a state of near sleep. "It's understandable that you're tired."

"Where did you go?" I asked, doing my best to stay awake. "After, I mean."

"Tried to wrap up the case on Peter." Maka shifted positions, allowing me to relax more comfortable in the cradle of his arm, head resting on his shoulder. "We followed as many leads as we could, traced the bank deposits. Unfortunately, we weren't able to connect a damn thing to Delgado. Everything was wrapped up clean, with nothing incriminating pointing his way. Looks like it was just Peter."

"He confessed to the money coming from Delgado."

"No, he confessed to someone paying him money to find out information *on* Delgado. There's no way to prove it was him, and he has politically powerful friends. This is as far as the investigation goes, unfortunately."

"But surely Peter knows—"

"Peter's dead," Maka said, voice quieter now.

I froze. The news caught me off guard, though I knew it shouldn't have surprised me. He was shot, after all, in the chest. Hell, as far as I knew he'd died right in front of my eyes. Funny how the thought never crossed my mind before that moment, though. I guess after someone confesses to murder right in front of you and then tries to kill you, your level of concern for their well-being is somewhat diminished.

"I heard gunfire," Maka said, like he had to explain to me. "I went in, saw him with the gun, saw you there... I shot him. I did my job."

I caught his face in my hands, tugging him down until he leaned forward and kissed him deeply. "I know. You did the right thing. Like I said before, you saved my life and Grace's. I just hate that Delgado is going to get away with it." I could just imagine Delgado's smug face as he saw his accomplice go down in flames while he himself remained unscathed.

Maka kissed my forehead. "Me too. That's why I'm going to pay him one last visit tomorrow. He'll have heard about Peter by then, so hopefully he'll have his guard down and will slip up. Not a big chance, but there's still a small one. Might as well give it a shot."

"I'm going, too," I said immediately. "After everything, I want to look him in the eyes one more time. Please? You have to admit I came in handy earlier."

"I'm too tired to argue with you tonight," Maka conceded. "You can come, but this time I need you to actually stay quiet, not just say you will and then ignore it."

"Okay, okay, if it'll get me in there, I promise."

I settled my head back on his shoulder, closing my eyes, letting his breathing soothe me back to sleep. Just as I was about to drift off, though, his hand came down hard on my ass, jarring me awake.

"Ow! What the hell was that for?"

"How many times since Friday have you almost been killed? I told you to be careful; you told me you would be, and you end up with a gun pointed in your face *again*. How is that even possible? How is one person *that* unlucky?"

"You say unlucky, I say lucky, since I'm still alive after every attempt," I said, a sleepy attempt at levity. He slapped the other ass cheek—not quite as hard as the first, but enough to make me hiss. "Ouch!"

"I'm serious, Gabe!"

"I blame Grace entirely," I grumbled. "She's the one that dragged my ass out here in the first place, so she started it all."

"Wait, wait, let's not get hasty," Maka said, cupping the same cheek he'd slap a moment before. "I like that your ass is here—the rest of you, too, but right now, particularly your ass."

"Well, you'll just have to demonstrate later just how much you like it being here," I said with a yawn. "But right now, I really need to go to sleep."

"Aw." Maka gave my ass a squeeze. "That's too bad."

I nuzzled closer to his neck, feeling safe and content. "I'll make it up to you later. Or let you make it up to me, whichever."

Maka laughed, the sound vibrating against my cheek, and that was the last thing I remembered before darkness claimed me again.

THE NEXT MORNING we made our way back to DLC Construction's main office, where Maka warned me again about being quiet when we were with Delgado. When we entered the building, Maka didn't bother stopping by the receptionist's desk, making a beeline for the elevator instead. When the receptionist hurried toward the elevator to stop us, Maka held down the "close" button until it did so.

"That was cold," I said appreciatively.

"I don't have time for the runaround today," Maka said tersely.

When the elevator doors opened on the eleventh floor we were greeted by Ashburn, no doubt thanks to the security cameras in the place. Just like before, he wore a three-piece suit. "You do not have permission to be here. You need to leave, immediately, before I call security."

"What's wrong?" Maka challenged, stepping up close to the well-dressed assistant and staring him down. Much to my surprise, Ashburn didn't so much as blink, even though a man of Maka's build would be intimidating for most people. "We just want to have a word with your boss, that's all."

"You've already taken up plenty of my boss's time," Ashburn said coldly. "Mr. Delgado is far too busy to deal with the likes of *you*."

"The likes of us?" Maka pretended to be stabbed in the chest. "You wound me."

"It's okay, Tyson." Delgado poked his head out of his office door. "I have a little free time in my schedule for the detective and his...friend. I'm sure this won't take too long."

Ashburn scowled but stepped aside. His eyes were particularly hate-filled when they settled on me, for some reason. Those eyes jarred something within me, the inklings of a memory, but they flicked away before I could fully recall it.

"I hear that you caught the person responsible for the death you claim is connected to me," Delgado said, holding the door open for Maka and me. "I am very happy to hear it. Our streets are safer thanks to the hard work of the Honolulu Police Department. I'm guessing it's too much to hope you've come to offer me an apology today?"

"Actually, we've come because the person responsible claimed to be doing it after being paid by you," Maka said bluntly. "A very specific amount, as well. Would you know anything about the transfer of twenty-one thousand dollars, Mr. Delgado?"

Delgado let out a long-suffering sigh. "As I told you before, Detective Kekoa, I know absolutely nothing about this guy."

"I think it's time for you to leave," Ashburn said, walking up behind Maka and grabbing his shoulder with his right hand. Maka reacted immediately, grasping Ashburn by the wrist, tightly. I caught Ashburn's wince of pain and looked closer at his eyes.

"Holy shit," I gasped.

"Take your hand off of me," Maka growled, thrusting Ashburn's hand away.

"Now, now, gentlemen, calm down," Delgado said, though he didn't sound that concerned with it.

"It was you," I said, pushing past Maka and striding up to Ashburn. "In my apartment and then at the photography store. That was you!"

"I don't have any idea what you're talking about," Ashburn said, drawing himself up and tugging at his tie nervously. But I wasn't wrong. Those eyes, those cold, merciless eyes, they were the same ones that stared out at me the previous day, behind a gun.

"I think you do." I grabbed Ashburn's wrist, squeezing it purposefully. "Does that hurt?"

"Gabe, stop!"

"Why does your arm hurt?" I went on, not letting go. "Is it because I bit you yesterday?"

"Excuse me?" Ashburn tried to pull away from me, but I wouldn't let him.

"I must insist you take your hand off my assistant."

"Gabe, what are you doing?" Maka sounded concerned and a little bit angry.

"Maka, this is the guy who broke into my apartment and attacked me at the photography place!"

"I did no such thing!"

"I can prove it," I insisted, maintaining my grip as Ashburn struggled to pull away from me. "When I was attacked yesterday, I bit the guy's wrist. Ashburn flinched when you grabbed his wrist—the same wrist I bit!"

Delgado came around his desk, his eyes hooded, but he said nothing.

"Show me your wrist," Maka demanded, switching immediately into his detective voice. "Now, Mr. Ashburn."

"I don't have to do any such thing," Ashburn huffed.

"Do it, Tyson," Delgado said. Something in his words brought a visible change in Ashburn; his body relaxed and a relaxed expression came over his face. He pulled free of my grip, unbuttoning the cuffs and rolling them back, exposing a nasty bruise and the clear imprints of teeth.

"I bet if we ran a test, it would match Mr. Maxfield's dental records here," Maka said, muscle in his jaw clenching.

"There will be no need for tests, Detective. I am confessing." The sudden change in Ashburn's attitude surprised me. Where did all of his vigorous protesting of his innocence go? Was it just because I exposed the bite mark? Or was there something more involved? I glanced at Delgado's face as Ashburn confessed, but it was a perfect expression of surprise. He was a damn good actor, I'd give him that.

"I did indeed break into Mr. Maxfield's apartment, and I did assault him at the photography shop. I was also the person who called Carrie Lange in order to convince her to cease her investigation of my boss."

"Tyson," Delgado gasped. "Why? You know as well as I do that she would have turned up nothing."

I doubt that, I thought, but managed to suppress the scoff; I didn't think it was the proper time.

"It could have hurt business if someone found out that you were being trailed. I was protecting you."

"And the money?"

"That was mine. I paid Peter myself. Mr. Delgado in no way authorized it and was in no way involved."

Delgado sat down on the corner of his desk, shaking his head. "Tyson, you fool."

Maka pulled a pair of handcuffs out of his inner jacket pocket. "Tyson Ashburn, you're under arrest..."

After Maka pushed Ashburn into the backseat of his car and closed the door, he gave me an apologetic look. "Are you sure you're okay waiting for Grace here? Unfortunately, you can't ride in with me if I have someone in custody."

"I'm fine. She'll be here soon. You go take him in." I kissed Maka gently. "Do you believe him? That Delgado wasn't involved?"

Maka shrugged. "Hard to say. I wouldn't be surprised if he kept things at a distance so they couldn't be connected to him. I don't know how much money Delgado would be giving him to keep his name out of it. I have no idea how long it'll be before I get home. I'll see you later."

Maka kissed me again and drove off.

God, I hope Grace doesn't take too long. I watched the taillights disappear from sight. It felt strange, standing out there in front of Delgado's office building. The hair on the back of my neck stood on end, and I felt eyes watching me. Glancing around, I saw no one. I looked back toward the building and saw Manuel Delgado standing just inside the doors, hands behind his back, watching me intently.

For a moment, I thought he would approach me and wondered if my life was in danger, but then Grace's Jeep pulled up in front of me. "Get in. I don't want to be here any longer than I have to be," she called.

"Are you okay?" she asked as I sat down and buckled my seat belt.

"I'm fine," I said offhandedly, glancing back toward the entrance to DLC Construction. Delgado was nowhere to be seen.

THE STORY OF what happened was a huge news sensation—local private eye and friend solve murder case—how could it not be?—and took several days to blow over. Both Grace and I decided to lay low for a bit, not wanting to have a bunch of cameras shined on us or questions thrown at us.

A week after our incident in the Paradise Investigations office, Grace asked to take me out to lunch. Things had died down, the news cycle beginning to let go of our story, so I thought why not, and she offered to pick me up.

We made small talk on the way to whatever restaurant. It felt good to just spend time together, not having to wonder about finding evidence to clear her name, or who did it. It wasn't all over, of course; Delgado was still free, but Peter was off the streets.

As we talked, I didn't pay any attention to where we were going, so when Grace brought the car to a stop, I fully expected it to be in front of some restaurant—which was good, because I was starving.

"Uh, Grace," I said, looking at where she'd brought me. "This isn't a restaurant."

She'd stopped the car in the parking lot of a small house converted into a business office. The sign in front of it read "Kei Paoa, DDS". Under that was a sign that said "For Sale."

"Looking to go into dentistry?" I asked wryly.

"Don't be an ass." Grace turned the car off and got out. "We'll get lunch in a sec. I just wanted to show this place to you."

"To me? Why?" I followed behind her.

"Isn't it perfect?"

"Perfect for what?"

"Listen, I can't stay in that office building anymore. Like you said, it was inconveniently located, and here, right on a major road where traffic gets busy, it will be much more suitable for drawing in clientele."

"Right, and this has nothing to do with the fact that your business partner was murdered in the old office, and you and I *almost* murdered." I didn't move fast enough to dodge Grace's punch, and my shoulder stung from the blow.

"Didn't I say don't be an ass?"

"Sorry. So why am *I* here?"

"Because I want you to become my new business partner. I can't afford the down payment on this place alone. Together we can buy it and reestablish Paradise Investigations. And don't say you can't because you're not a licensed detective—because I am, and only one of us needs to be. You can get your license over time."

"Grace," I started, but the look she gave me made me stop. "Why do you want to keep doing this after everything that happened?"

"I'm good at this, Gabe. I make a good private investigator—you do, too, judging by last weekend."

"My brief foray into private investigating resulted in me almost being choked to death, almost being shot, and then almost being shot again," I reminded her.

"Anomalies," she said dismissively. "Besides, it *also* got you in bed with one extremely sexy Hawaiian detective, right? See, look at that smile. You know I'm right. Come on, this way you can be your own boss—and make money, to boot. I know it's not a fancy paralegal position at a high-powered law office, but you'd get to work with me and see this beautiful face every day." She held her hands up, framing her face for emphasis. "That's better than writing law briefs and filing motions and whatever it is you did in Seattle, right? Come on," she begged, grabbing my hand and tugging it. "You came here for a new start, right? What better way to start new than in an entirely new career?"

I looked into her hopeful face and felt my resolve crumbling. What else did I have to do with my time? *Maka's going to* hate *this idea.* "You should have become a salesperson," I said, and she let out a loud whoop of celebration, pumping her fist in the air.

"Wait, wait—I set my own hours, right?"

Grace nodded.

"We decide *together* what cases to take—none of this separate and no information nonsense that you and Carrie hard, right?"

Another nod.

"Okay, I'm in."

Grace grabbed my hand and tugged me toward the office of Kei Paoa, DDS, soon to be the office of Paradise Investigations, chattering about the inside and how nice it was and how many ideas she had about how to set it up and make it work perfectly.

This is going to be a terrible idea, I thought with certainty, a small smile on my face. *But at least it will be a fun one.*

About the Author

J. C. Long is an American expat living in Japan, though he's also lived stints in Seoul, South Korea—no, he's not an army brat; he's an English teacher. He is also quite passionate about Welsh corgis and is convinced that anyone who does not like them is evil incarnate. His dramatic streak comes from his lifelong involvement in theatre. After living in several countries aside from the United States, J. C. is convinced that love is love, no matter where you are, and he is determined to write stories that demonstrate exactly that. J. C. Long's favorite things in the world are pictures of corgis, writing, and Korean food (not in that order...okay, in that order). J. C. spends his time when not writing by thinking about writing, coming up with new characters, attending Big Bang concerts, and wishing he was writing. The best way to get him to write faster is to motivate him with corgi pictures. Yes, that is a veiled hint.

Facebook: https://www.facebook.com/authorjclong
Twitter: @j_c_long_author
Website: http://www.jclong.org/
Email:jclongauthor@gmail.com

Also by J.C. Long

Unzipped Shorts
New Year's Eve Unzipped
Unzipping 7D

Hong Kong Nights
A Matter of Duty

Coming Soon from J.C. Long

A Matter of Courage

Hong Kong Nights, Books 2

Blurb

Winston Chang has spent much of his young life admiring the Dragons who have kept his area safe and fought off the gangs that would bring violence to their area. Now that he's an adult he wants nothing more than to join the Dragons and live up to those standards.

The opportunity presents itself when his passion and knowledge of cars is just what the Dragons need. One of their own has been killed and his death seems linked to his involvement with the illegal racing scene known as the Dark Streets. Winston is needed to infiltrate the scene and find out who is responsible and why.

Steel has always been Winston's best friend, and Winston has always been there to get him out of trouble. Just as the stress in Winston's life reaches its peak, the relationship between Winston and Steel begins to change in ways neither of them expected.

Will Winston and Steel be able to find the courage to face not only the unknown killer stalking the Dark Streets racers, but also their growing feelings?

Also Available from NineStar Press

www.ninestarpress.com